THE AVENGERS

DEAD DUCK

PATRICK MACNEE

Titan Books
LONDON

THE AVENGERS: DEAD DUCK
ISBN 1 85286 562 8

Published by
Titan Books Ltd
42-44 Dolben Street
London SE1 0UP

First Titan edition September 1994
10 9 8 7 6 5 4 3 2 1

British Library Cataloguing-in-Publication Data. A catalogue record for this book is available from the British Library.

Copyright © 1966 by Patrick Macnee and Peter Leslie.
The Avengers © 1961-8 Lumiere Pictures Ltd.

This book is sold subject to the condition that it shall not by way of trade or otherwise, be lent, re-sold, hired out or otherwise circulated without the publisher's prior consent in any form of binding or cover other than that in which it is published and without a similar condition including this condition being imposed upon the subsequent purchaser.

Printed and bound by Cox and Wyman Ltd, Reading, Berkshire.

For a complete list of all Titan's Film and TV publications, please send a large stamped SAE to Titan Books Mail Order, 42-44 Dolben Street, London SE1 0UP. Please quote reference A2 on both envelopes.

CONTENTS

Chapter		Page
1	The Death of Three	7
2	An Interrupted Meal	12
3	Steed Smells a Rat ...	18
4	Hearts Come Up Trumps!	23
5	"It looks like one of ours."	31
6	The Corpse In The Cardboard Coffin	36
7	Enter a Girl With a Shotgun!	44
8	Conversation With a Poacher	49
9	Bella Goes To Work	58
10	The House On The Marsh	67
11	A Ghost In a Battered Bowler ...	80
12	Matters of Migration	88
13	Below Stairs For Emma ... ... And Steed In a Cupboard!	98
14	Exit a Journalist!	114
15	Operation Worthington	126
16	A Touch of the Sun	138
17	Mrs Peel Passes Out	147
18	You Can Always Duck ...	159

1

THE DEATH OF THREE

THROUGHOUT the morning, the tramp sat in the shelter of a blackthorn bush, facing the high storm-beach cutting off the view of the sea on the far side of the road. Behind him, tall reeds clattered and bent in a wind gusting inshore from the East.

The road appeared to one side of a clump of trees crowning a slight rise to the North, vanished briefly in a shallow dip and then arrowed southwards across the flat countryside for nearly two miles before it twisted out of sight round the grassed bank of a dyke. No other human being, no building broke the monotony of the featureless landscape, though birds shifted from branch to branch in the foliage behind the barrier of reeds and an occasional seagull soared momentarily into sight above the shingle ridge. Beyond the incessant, invisible surge of waves, no sound broke the moaning of the wind and the macadam stretched away empty and desolate on either side of the seated man. At his feet, a ring of stones from the beach preserved the ashes of a fire on the wide verge, on top of which a battered billycan held the remains of a meal. Beside a shabby bundle nearby, an enamel plate glinted in the pale sunlight.

Then, in the early afternoon, when the sun had risen far into the pale, clear sky and the shadow of the storm-beach had withdrawn from the road, a moving dot manifested itself on the horizon. Rapidly it approached down the incline, disappeared into the dip, rose into view again much nearer, resolved itself into a small tradesman's van and passed the tramp in a swirl of dust. Soon it was dwindling once more to a speck, to be cut off abruptly by the wall of the dyke.

The dust subsided; the roadside grasses resumed their leaning stance away from the inflexible wind. The tramp remained motionless, facing the blank mound of stones across the road.

Later a Jaguar hissed past on its way North, and before it was out of sight, a clergyman in an ancient Austin passed slowly in the opposite direction.

The sun crawled across the high sky. Slowly, inexorably, the shadows swept the grass, charting the passage of the day. Flights of wild geese in formation flew out to sea, calling hoarsely, as a bank of cloud blew up behind the shingle mass.

When the sun had crossed the road and was sinking behind the distant dyke, seven army lorries in close convoy thundered past towards the North, hugging the side of the road. The wind of their passage threshed the branches of the blackthorn and tossed the reeds behind the seated man. As the birds startled from their perches by the din settled protestingly down again, he leaned slowly forwards and pitched to the ground, his sightless eyes buried in the cold ashes of the fire.

* * *

A half hour later, as the olive-drab convoy roared through the village of Bratby in the gathering dusk, the driver of the leading vehicle swore, flashed his headlamps, stamped on the heavy brake pedal, and then swerved desperately in an attempt to miss the small saloon which persisted in edging out from the side road across his path.

The big lorry slewed sideways in the narrow street, clipped the high curb on the offside, bounced back into the middle of the road and turned completely round, the covered tail smashing into the *Keep Left* bollard of an island refuge and snapping off the pole of a street lamp behind it. There was a vivid blue flash, and the whole length of Bratby High Street was plunged into gloom. Before the scream of brakes from the following members of the convoy had died away, the driver of the leading vehicle and his mate had wrenched open their doors, dropped to the ground, and were sprinting across the broken glass towards the car which had caused the accident.

"Crazy bastard!" the driver panted as he ran. "Crawling out of a ruddy side street with no lights on like that! I'll show the bleedin'—"

"Hasn't even stopped, for Chrissake," gasped his mate. *"Look!"*

The two men halted, staring, in the middle of the road.

The saloon had crossed the main road behind the crashing lorry, missing the gyrating tail by inches, and penetrated a narrow No Entry street opposite. Now, as they watched, it was moving away from them at a slow walking pace towards the lights of a small square at the far end of the one-way thoroughfare. Deliberately, almost caressingly, it scraped along the side of a parked Mercedes before veering to the other side of the road, mounting the pavement, and rasping itself along a brick wall. Through the rear window they could see the silhouette of the driver hunched over the wheel.

"Come on, mate," the driver said suddenly. "Something wrong here. Let's go . . ."

Together, the two men raced after the car. But before they caught up, it had entered the square. The driver appeared to lurch to one side, the exhaust note rose abruptly, and the little saloon leaped forward to crash with shattering force into a stone horse trough on the far side of the open space.

In the sudden silence after the appalling impact, the noise of the soldiers' boots pounding on the road sounded unnaturally loud. A piece of broken glass dislodged itself from somewhere and tinkled to the ground. Petrol from the saloon's ruptured tank splashed to the ground and spiced the chilly evening air with its aromatic tang.

Then windows were being thrust up in the timbered houses, voices called, people trooped into the street to join the other members of the convoy who had followed the driver and his mate. Before the soldiers reached the wrecked car, the square was echoing to the noise of many feet.

The driver yanked open the offside door. "Blimey," he cried, "I reckon this bloke's had it, and all . . ."

The middle aged man who had been the saloon's only occupant had been forced half through the fragmented windscreen by the crash. On the crumpled bonnet, his face lay pierced by wicked shards of glass. The thin steering column with its distorted wheel had torn the overcoat away from his right shoulder, so that this arm now splayed grotesquely behind him, a limp hand dangling from the lanced sleeve.

"Jesus," the driver's mate said. "Let's get him out of there. Hold the door open wider, Charlie. Wider . . . Come on, now, folks: give us a bit of room, will you? . . . There—thanks, mate: get a hold of that leg, would you? —easy does it. *Easy* . . . Look, for Chrissake let's have a bit of *room* . . ."

"All right, you people," the crisp voice of the sergeant in charge of the convoy spoke behind them. "Stand back there and give the bloke a chance. Lay him on the floor there, Foster. Gently now. You, Reed, strip off your jacket and put it under his head. That's it. Now . . ."—he swept the peering villagers with a glance—"... anyone here tell me where the local doctor lives?"

"He *is* the local doctor," someone volunteered.

"But he don't *live*," Foster, white-faced, spoke from the ground by the victim. "He's copped it, Sarn't. He's dead."

"Dead before the smash, too, I shouldn't wonder," the sergeant replied. "Hardly any blood, see? Though how the hell that car came all that way on its own..." His voice trailed away.

"Oh, it could, Sarn't," one of the other drivers said. "It's a Fiat 600, see. The wife's brother has one. They're so light, the engine'll drive 'em along in bottom without you touching the accelerator. If they're in gear, I mean."

"That must of been it," Foster said. "Then, when the car hit the wall, the body moved and his foot pressed the pedal and sent it roaring into this." He gestured at the stone trough.

"Heart attack, probably." The sergeant's voice became assured and authoritative again; all phenomena accounted for. "Still and all, we ought to get a doctor. Police, too. Anyone here got a phone?"

"Jamie's gone for the police," a woman said. "You can use my phone across the road there. The only other doctor around here's Maltby at Great Hornham. The number's two-one-seven."

As she led the sergeant across the road to the lighted doorway of a cottage, the villagers stood uncertainly around the crashed Fiat, embarrassed in the presence of death. Off to one side, the soldiers muttered among themselves in a separate group. The driver, Reed, stepped forward and knelt by the flat-tyred, buckled front wheel to spread a handkerchief over the dead man's lacerated face.

But Dr Maltby was out on a case, the sergeant found out when he telephoned. "He's over seeing that young woman, the painter, who lives in the Martello tower at Star Point," a woman told him in her soft East Coast accent. "If it's an emergency, you could get him there." She gave him a number.

The sergeant dialled again.

* * *

The phone rang as Dr Maltby was packing up his bag in the big, bare room in the converted tower. Canvases were stacked around the walls, propped against the cheap table, resting on easels. Most of them were landscapes—flat, low-key marsh scenes with water birds in the foreground. Wind stammered the small-paned windows in their frames and boomed in the stone stairway. The girl lay in a huge bed under the single oil lamp, her long gold hair spread fanwise on the pillow. A faded pair of blue jeans, inside out, had been dropped across a chair. Below, a paint-splotched sweater and a torn brassière were crumpled on the flagged floor.

The doctor's hands were trembling as he sought for the telephone among the books, jars of brushes, sheets of paper and twisted paint tubes in the shadowed reaches of the room.

"Yes?" he said absently, mopping his brow with a paint rag. "Yes, this is Maltby speaking . . . An accident, you say? In Bratby? . . . Doctor—why, that must be Atherley! Good God! How dreadful . . . Yes. Yes, of course I'll come . . . I'll be there as quickly as I can . . ."

He continued talking, half to himself, as he replaced the receiver.

"Most extraordinary thing I ever saw," he mumbled. "Fantastic. Nothing worse than a simple streptococcus infection of the pharynx . . . and then to collapse like that! It's not natural. Girl's heart was as sound as a bell . . . Checked on it myself less than an hour ago. And now another . . ."

He shook his head, picked up his bag and moved towards the door, hesitated, then sighed and crossed the room to the telephone again.

Behind him among the pillows, the girl's contorted face pointed rigidly at the high ceiling.

2

AN INTERRUPTED MEAL

"THE whole point about a good *sauce vinaigrette*," John Steed said, "is that it's a completely *personal* thing: you can't make it to a formula. It's your particular, private blend of oil, vinegar, salt, pepper and mustard that counts. That's what makes or mars it; any fool can hurl in the chopped capers or gherkins or parsley or whatever."

Across the table, Emma Peel smiled indulgently at him over the rim of her Suze. "Brillat-Savarin might disagree with your principle," she said, "and De Nobrega would certainly quarrel with the mustard—"

"There you *are*, you see!" Steed interrupted triumphantly. "That's just what I mean! Anyway—let's go and sample Mark's, shall we?"

Taking her solicitously by one elbow, he piloted the girl through the press of people thronging the aperitif bar towards the dining room.

The "Ely Cathedral" boasts a clientele considerably more recondite than its position or appearance would suggest. The inn lies at the foot of a steep hill between Little Hornham and Boston—an L-shaped 17th-century building of no particular architectural merit: lath-and-plaster, exposed beams and East Anglian thatch disposed agreeably enough in a curve of the river which winds towards the Wash. Its fishing is passable, its shooting negligible, the accommodation comfortable, if limited. Yet the small car park across the footbridge on the far side of the water is always jammed with machinery of the most expensive and récherché kind. Besides Steed's blown 4½-litre Bentley, there were on this particular evening a Ferrari, an Iso Rivolta, a brace of 2600 Alfas, a Matra-Bonnet Djet and a covey of Marcos GT's among the more pedestrian Rolls, Aston Martins and E-Types standing there—and the registration marks testified to journeys from as far afield as London, Chester, Shrewsbury and even Edinburgh...

The reason for this was simple: Mark Lurchman, the owner,

had learned to cook at the "Pyramide" in Vienne, that Rhône valley gastronomic shrine whose table earns it the coveted three rosettes in the *Guide Michelin*—one of only a dozen in the whole of France. And although the proprietor himself now rarely officiated in the kitchens, his influence was still strong enough to make the "Ely Cathedral" (in the words of the famous guide) well worth a detour.

The head waiter seated Steed and Emma at a corner table from which they could comfortably survey the rest of the panelled dining room. It wasn't large—a central dispense buffet with a superb cold table arranged on it, a ring of well spaced tables, and an alcove at each end—but everything in it was well chosen, well displayed and in perfect condition. There was a subdued hum of conversation, a discreet tinkling of silverware and fine china below the illumination welling softly outwards from concealed ports in the blackened ships' timbers which served as beams for the white ceiling. Behind Steed, the glass of a framed Morland engraving reflected the sudden flare of light from a trolley on the far side of the room where a pineapple *flambé* was being prepared.

Steed glanced at the picture as he shook his napkin free of its starched convolutions and dropped it across his knees. "Oh," he said, "I see Mark's managed to get the wildfowling one at last. Makes a good pair with the fishing scene on the other side of the alcove, don't you think? . . . I always wondered, though, why the coloured retainer was so much better dressed than the shooting party itself—and why on earth he's sitting on a kitchen chair in the middle of a skiff!"

"He probably brought it along because he knew very well he'd have to wait an age before he ate," Emma Peel murmured mischievously.

"My dear Mrs Peel! Do forgive me . . . One does run on, doesn't one? Now—to what Lucullan dish may I tempt you in expiation?"

The girl smiled at him once more across the table. In the diffuse top-lighting, her tawny hair glowed softly against the turquoise *lamé* of an evening trouser suit. Above the high cheekbones, her enormous brown eyes held Steed's ironic grey ones for a moment before she turned her attention to the menu. Daughter of a shipping magnate, widow of a supersonic test pilot, rich enough to be her own mistress and nobody else's,

Emma Peel was still zestful enough, at 27, to relish a dinner date with a civilised and charming companion.

"I see they have leeks *vinaigrettes*," she said. "After your dissertation, no self-respecting woman could avoid choosing them. As for the rest, though—since you brought me all the way out here just because the food was so good, I think it's only fair that you should be allowed to select whatever dishes you feel can justify the journey!"

"A challenge!" Steed said. "Right. There's a bottle of Alsatian Tokay—fruity but very dry—cooling for us. A bottle of Grands Echézeaux should have been opened in here half an hour ago ... yes, there it is over there on the sideboard, look. I suggest that we have a simple *truite aux amandes* with the former, and Mark's speciality for tonight with the Burgundy."

"What is the speciality?"

"Duck *à la Rouennaise*," Steed said impressively. "You don't often get it in England, and it should be pretty good here."

"I'm terribly sorry, Steed," Emma said contritely, "but I don't know what it is."

"Splendid! That'll give me the chance to tell you. It's a—"

"Mr Steed! How very nice! Welcome back, welcome back ..." The deep voice interrupted from over the waiter's shoulder. The owner of the "Ely Cathedral" was short, wide, brick-red faced and very dark, with a great blade of a nose flanked by twinkling, bright blue eyes.

"Hallo, Mark," Steed said, rising to his feet and introducing Emma. "Much of Mrs Peel's education was on the continent and in South America. I felt it my duty to demonstrate that we could still teach her something here—even if it was only in the culinary arts."

"Excellent, excellent," chuckled the man with the deep voice. "Though I take grave exception to that word 'only'. Now what are you going to have?" He leaned over the waiter's arm and scrutinised the order pencilled on his pad. "Ah, yes—the *poireaux*, trout with almonds ... Good! ... and the *Canard à la Rouennaise*. Fine."

"Mr Steed was about to initiate me into the mysteries of this dish," Emma said. "I'm afraid I don't know it at all."

"Why should you, dear lady? Why should you?" Lurchman said. "But however accomplished your host, this is a task I must arrogate to myself—you will permit me, Mr Steed?"

"Go ahead, Mark: you're the professional," Steed smiled. He

AN INTERRUPTED MEAL

leaned back in his chair and looked idly at his fellow diners. There were several tables of solid, respectable-looking elderly folk—business people from Lincoln or Ely, or academics and their wives from Cambridge, he guessed. At the far end of the room, six lively young Italians were joking with the waiter heating their *shashlick* on skewers. A well-known television actor was psychoanalysing himself for the breathless benefit of a very young blonde. Two fat men talking French were slowly swilling Armagnac around the tulip glasses cupped in their hands. Nearer, two stridently "county" women in tweeds were extolling the virtues either of a stallion or a male acquaintance —Steed couldn't quite make out which. Their escorts stared mournfully at each other's moustaches across the white tablecloth.

Steed shifted his glance past the table next to his own—a tall man with glasses was sitting alone, wolfing a plateful of something covered in white sauce—to Lurchman and Emma. As an undercover man, one of those most special of agents not even assigned to a specific department, he was forced to use his man-of-the-world charm as a cloak for a particular type of ruthless dedication. To Steed, the end always justified the means—and if the means sometimes required a certain callousness, a certain unscrupulousness in the deployment of this charm to co-opt the assistance of such "amateur" help as Emma, well, that was all part of the game.

Even so, in those rare moments when he was, as it were, "off duty", Steed normally preserved an identical detachment towards his helpers. Tonight, though . . . he looked across at the square jawline, the imperious tilt of the triangular, pointed chin, the sensitivity of the wide mouth, as Emma listened, appreciatively to Lurchman's peroration . . . tonight even Steed's iron nerves could not stifle a quickening of the pulse as his eye took in a voluptuous curve of the *lamé* jacket below the hollow of the shoulder, snatched a glimpse of a matching brassière between its open buttons, and lingered on a taut plane of suntanned flesh above the tight belt of the hipster trousers. Whichever way you looked at it—and it was equally pleasant any way!—Emma Peel was a very beautiful young woman . . .

". . . after it's been roasting twenty minutes," Mark Lurchman was saying, "you cut off the breast in long, thin slices, disjoint the legs and wings, and leave the whole shoot on one side while you attend to the carcass."

"I'm fascinated," Emma said, catching Steed's eye.

"That's when your special press comes in," Lurchman continued. "And that's why you'll rarely get the dish—or Duckling *á la Duclair* for that matter—in this country. You crush the carcass in this press and collect the blood, add the rest of the blood you have, deglaze it with red wine, and make a sauce with the blood, the duck's liver, and a couple of onions. Then, when the sauce has been reduced, you thicken it with butter and add the bits of the bird you've put on one side—simmering the lot until it's done."

"Fabulous. You can see why the English were always trying to take back Rouen from the French," Emma murmured.

The proprietor laughed his fat laugh again. "By the time we've put in our own stuffing and added the special *croutons*," he said, "you will see why Mr Steed enthuses. *Bon appetit, madame* . . ." He waved his hand and drifted across the dining room to talk to the Italians.

Later, when the exquisite trout was but a memory and the Tokay a tune vibrating in it, they watched with unconcealed interest as a waiter wheeled up a trolley and served Duck *à la Rouennaise* to the solitary man at the next table. His spectacles glinted greedily as he bent low over the spirit heater, drinking in every detail of the entrée dish sizzling on top of it. He inhaled appreciatively above the thick, rich, brown cargo of sauce, with its slivers of flesh savourily awash. He rubbed his hands with anticipation as the *croutons* were arranged on his plate and the contents of the dish reverently disbursed over them. And he exclaimed aloud with pleasure as the first morsel passed his lips.

Emma raised her eyebrows and turned back to Steed.

"Your proprietorial friend seems not to be the only enthusiast for the dish," she observed drily.

"Ours will be here in a moment; you'll see," Steed promised her with a grin. He waved away the wine waiter, who was offering to pour him a taste of the Grands Echézeaux. "I'm absolutely certain, my dear fellow," he said, "that Mark would never dream of charging *his* prices for anything that was less than perfect! You may pour . . ."

Emma sipped the lustrous Burgundy. "I must agree—it is rather gorgeous," she said reflectively. "Heavy and round-flavoured and rich. Now tell me, Steed: what are you up to? Why are we here?"

The undercover man rolled the wine around his mouth and

AN INTERRUPTED MEAL

swallowed. "Perfect," he said. "Perfect. I've heard it described as having 'a violent bouquet of cherries and violets'. I can't say I can see that at all ... To me, it simply tastes splendidly, beautifully, caressingly of *wine*! What were you saying, my dear?"

"I asked you to come clean—and tell me why we're here."

"But to eat and drink, of course ... Why else?"

"Oh, Steed! Please! Do I have to wait for the coffee?"

The faint, sardonic smile vanished from the agent's square-ish face. Above the impeccable dark suit, the clean lines of his features gathered under the crisp, dark hair into a frown. He looked for once slightly at a loss. "Mrs Peel," he began, "I do assure you—how can I convince ... " He broke off, raised his eyes towards the ceiling, and started again. "Look," he said, "for once we're here *without* an ulterior motive! Honestly. I just thought you'd like to try the food."

"I'm sorry, Steed. I simply do not believe you."

"But I give you my word—"

"In cases like this, your word's only as good as the next national emergency. Come on—what is it this time?"

"Oh, now *really*—" Steed began.

"Sorry, Mr Steed," a passing waiter called. "Be with you in a minute. Won't keep you another moment ..."

"Quite all right," Steed called back. "We're not *pressés*, even if the duck is ... Now look here, young woman—"

"It won't wash, Steed. It won't wash. I mean, I don't *mind*: it's just that I will not have my intelligence insulted."

"But I tell you ..." The undercover man sat back with a sigh that was part amusement, part exasperation. "What can I say to you?"

"Just tell me *why* we're here," Emma said. "All right—the food is admirable; the wine is all you said it would be. But I simply cannot believe you'd come all this way for that alone. There must be another reason. Things have a habit of—happening, shall we say?—when you're around."

Exploding into the quiet sounds of dinner, a chair crashed over backwards. The tall man at the next table was on his feet, scrabbling at his chest with frenzied hands. A high, whinnying noise forced itself from his lips. He belched loudly and jackknifed forwards, to sprawl face downwards among the plates and glasses with an impact that shook the room.

"You see what I mean?" Emma Peel said.

3

STEED SMELLS A RAT...

THE rain had stopped now and the East wind was scudding low clouds across the half moon. In the churned up mud of the car park, only Steed's vast vintage Bentley, Mark Lurchman's E-Type Jaguar and an old Austin belonging to the doctor remained under the dripping trees.

They had tried artificial respiration, they had tried injections, they had tried oxygen, coramine and other stimulants—but the tall man with the glasses was unmistakably, definitively and permanently dead. At last, the ambulance from Great Hornham had taken him away, leaving Emma Peel, Steed, Lurchman and the doctor grouped under the back porch of the "Ely Cathedral" rather like the bride and groom's parents after the honeymoon car has departed.

The doctor had actually been in the bar when the victim collapsed. He had been on the scene almost as soon as Steed had got the man lying flat and loosened his collar and tie. And he had sprinted over the bridge across the river, opened up the boot of his car and run back with the necessary equipment before a couple of minutes had passed.

But they had both known, as they worked together waiting for the ambulance, that it was too late.

"Obviously a sudden syncope—a cardiac failure," the doctor had said to Steed. He was a small man with a bald head and a stubby moustache. "Symptoms are obvious, so far as I can see: the clammy skin, the beads of perspiration, the cyanosed lips. Can't tell why, of course, as I wasn't here when it happened. Could be Angina. A coronary—no way of telling without some knowledge of the patient, whether there's a history of D.A.H., and so on . . ."

"D.A.H.?"

"Disorderly action of the heart," the little doctor explained.

"I see. Would anyone around here know about that?"

"Shouldn't think so. Fellow's a stranger, you see. Staying here for a few days. Just arrived in a cab from the station and took a room. Lurchman told me."

"What do you do about the Death Certificate, then?" Emma had asked.

"Do, young lady? Do? Why nothing, of course. Can't do a thing in the circumstances. Not enough to go on, you see. Have to do a P.M., have an inquest, contact the fellow's own G.P. and so on."

"And who'll conduct the post-mortem?"

"Well, as a matter of fact I shall have to. My name's Maltby, by the way. Gregory Maltby."

"How d'you do, Doctor Maltby? I'm Emma Peel. And this is John Steed."

They had murmured the usual inanities and then Steed had asked, in a conversational way, if Maltby encountered any difficulties in such cases with his local coroner. There had been an awkward pause. The doctor had coughed and reddened slightly.

"Well—it's an extraordinary thing," he had said at last, "but in fact I'm the coroner, too. Or at least I think so . . ."

"I don't quite understand."

"Well—er—it's Atherley . . . it *was* Atherley, I should have said. That is to say my colleague is—was—the coroner, but he was killed in an accident today."

"I'm sorry."

"So, as I'm the only other candidate around here, I suppose at least temporarily . . ." His voice had trailed off. And then: "But it's odd, damned odd," he had said. "I simply do not understand . . ."

"What don't you understand, Doctor Maltby?"

"Nothing, nothing . . . Never mind," the little man had said gruffly. And he had bustled off almost immediately afterwards on some pretext or other—something about getting the spelling of the dead man's name right from the hotel register.

The only thing was, the dead man hadn't signed the register. He had apparently arrived that afternoon, promised the receptionist that he would attend to the matter before dinner, and forgotten to do so. Odder still was the fact that among the effects in his clothes—watch, wallet, engagement diary, money, keys, cigarettes and lighter, a couple of circulars put out by local building societies—there was not a single item with a name or an address on it. Nor could Steed discover any when he slipped upstairs unseen and turned-over the dead man's room briefly but expertly while the body was being loaded into the ambulance. There were laundry marks and dry-cleaning codes on the clothes, of course. It would be a comparatively easy matter to identify the mysterious guest in time. But for the moment he would remain a corpse strictly anonymous. And it looked very much as though he himself had planned it that way.

"I suppose," Steed said now, as the four of them stood in the porch watching the lights of the ambulance fade away among the trees, "I suppose there isn't any remote chance that the food could have had anything to do with his death?"

"The *food*, Mr Steed!" Mark Lurchman sounded scandalised.

"Certainly not," Maltby snapped. "I told you: he died of a heart attack. Can't be sure which of the various cardiac conditions *caused* the failure, as I said. But there's no doubt at all that it *was* heart failure. None whatever." He turned abruptly and barged through the swing door into the interior of the inn.

"I didn't mean there was anything wrong with the food, Mark," Steed said mildly. "I was just wondering—I mean, perhaps some allergy ... maybe some ingredient in one of the dishes ... " He gestured vaguely. "The chap was certainly cramming it in at a prodigious rate of knots."

"So the waiter told me," Lurchman admitted, mollified.

"Would the remains of the food have been kept, Mark?" Steed persisted. "I mean, I know half the glasses and crockery were smashed when he fell, but what about the entrée dish itself, for example?"

The owner of the "Ely Cathedral" looked away. "No ... No, I'm afraid not," he said evasively. "I tell you it was all thrown away. You can't blame the staff—it was chaos in there for a while. Naturally they cleared it all up. There were other guests to consider."

"All right, old lad. All right," Steed soothed. "I only wondered."

He turned and went back into the hotel, ushering Emma before him.

"Mr Steed, Mr Steed!" The head waiter was covered in confusion. "You were helping so much, you never get the rest of your meal. Please! Let me make something now for you and for Madame?"

"Thank you, Giorgio, I really don't think ..." the undercover man began. Then he paused, struck by a thought. "Wait a minute, though," he said slowly. "The Duck *à la Rouennaise* that was being prepared for us. Presumably it's still there? Couldn't you heat that up for us?"

"Oh, Mr Steed, it wouldn't be the same. You know it wouldn't."

"Yes, Steed," Emma said quickly. "I really don't feel I could . . ."

"Have a look, Giorgio, will you?" the agent continued smoothly.

He waited, blandly aloof, until the man came back, a puzzled frown puckering his round, sallow face. "Is a funny thing, Mr Steed," he said. "It seems to have dissappear. Maybe one of the boys throw it out by mistake, eh?"

"Not by mistake, I fancy," Steed said softly. "But never mind. No—I wouldn't dream of having you make us another one, thank you. Come to think of it, I'm a bit off duck for to-night, anyway! Besides we must be getting back to town. On the other hand, there *is* the rest of that Echézeaux—I trust *that* hasn't been—er—thrown away?"

"Mr *Steed*!"

"No? I'm relieved to hear it, Giorgio . . . In that case, let us have some cheese—say a Chalaronne or a Géramont—and we'll polish it off."

But it was not until they were thundering home with the Bentley's touring hood up that he confided to Emma what he had seen from the window of the dead man's bedroom while he was searching it.

"It was still raining then," he said. "Absolutely pelting down. I happened to glance down into the garden as I crossed the room from the dressing table to the wardrobe—and there was this girl, waiting on the far side of the little bridge across the river."

"What kind of girl?" Emma asked, interested.

"The kind the Italians respectfully call *robusta*. You know— good, round arms, sturdy legs, billowy hips and tiny waist, with those huge, firm breasts that seem to go with that sort of figure."

"That must have been quite a glance."

Steed smiled. "You could hardly have avoided it," he said. "She was wearing a cheap cotton frock with no raincoat, and the material was plastered to that body by the rain and wind as though it was just drawn on."

"What kind of a face did she have? How old was she?"

"I only saw her for a moment, as somebody opened a door downstairs and she was outlined for a second in a shaft of light.

Besides, she had long hair and it was all stuck to her face by the weather. But she seemed to be the, you know, the sort of gypsy type."

"The proud animal, on equal terms with the elements?"

"Not quite as Mary Webb as that. Besides, she can't have been a day over nineteen. And she looked as scared as all get-out!"

"But what was she *doing* there, Steed?"

"I soon found that out. She was obviously waiting—but impatient to be away. Anyway, in a few seconds a man in a black slicker crept furtively along the path from the porch to the bridge, looked right and left, and then crossed the bridge to meet her."

"And then?"

"He pulled some kind of a package from under his raincoat, thrust it into her hands, and she vanished into the bushes like a dose of salts!"

"What did he do?"

"Hurried back to the pub as quickly as he could."

"Did you see who it was, Steed?"

"Yes. He crossed a bar of light from some window just before he reached the porch. It was Mark."

Emma gave a low whistle, clearly audible over the burble of the Bentley's two-and-a-half-inch exhaust as they rolled through Braintree. "I'm sorry I doubted your word earlier on, Steed," she said. "You're obviously as astonished by tonight's goings-on as I have been. What an odd sequence of events!"

"I think it's a bit more than odd, to tell the truth," Steed replied. "One way or another, I small a rat. A rat with wings..."

4

HEARTS COME UP TRUMPS!

NEWSPAPERS were scattered all over the three wide stairs linking the two levels of Steed's sitting room when Emma Peel arrived at the flat in Westminster Mews the next morning. Her host, resplendent in a waisted lovat-green suit with a velvet collar, was perched on the edge of a wine-and-gold striped Regency settee, leaning forward with his forearms resting on his elegant knees as he gazed reflectively down at the litter of newsprint. Three items on a trio of separate pages were ringed in red marker pencil.

"Good morning, Steed," Emma called cheerfully. "The door was open, so I came up. What are you doing—trying your fancy for the two-thirty?"

Steed rose to his feet and helped his visitor off with her coat—a black wool affair braided in black and white, which concealed a white wool dress braided in black, rather like a photograph and its negative.

"Nothing so lively, I'm afraid," he replied with a smile. "All the subjects of this little investigation are strictly non-runners."

"These?" She indicated the papers on the steps. "Anything to do with our unfortunate friend last night?"

"Perhaps. I'm not quite sure yet," Steed said with a puzzled frown. "I went out to get the nationals and some locals, just in case. But the man from the 'Ely Cathedral' hasn't made any of them. On the other hand . . ." He paused, then picked up the three marked copies and handed them to her. "Have a look for yourself," he said soberly.

Emma glanced at each of the three papers in turn, then looked up enquiringly, her dark eyebrows raised.

"Don't you see anything odd about them?" Steed asked.

"One from the *Gazette,* one from the *East Anglian Echo,* one from the *Lincoln Mercury*—no, I don't think so." She examined the ringed stories in more detail. "Apart from the fact that they all report deaths in one way or another, nothing strikes me. They're all different people."

"But they don't all report deaths 'in one way or another'—they report deaths in the same way."

"Oh, surely not, Steed: one's a straight obituary; one's a news story about a man killed in a car crash; one's an announcement about a new speaker for a political meeting—mentioning by the way that the change has been occasioned by the death of the man originally down to talk."

"Yes, yes, my dear. The manner of *reporting's* different—but the *deaths*, the manner of death ... What about that?"

"Oh. Yes—I see what you mean. All heart failure. And so?"

"And all taking place ...?" Steed insisted.

Emma hesitated. She looked at the newspaper stories again. "That *is* strange," she admitted slowly at last. "The car crash at Bratby, the painter at Star Point, the orator at Great Hornham ... and, of course, the poor chap we saw last night: they're all within a few miles of each other."

"Exactly."

"But that's not all, Steed!"

"What d'you mean—that's not all?"

The girl fumbled in her handbag. "Of course, it *may* be simply a coincidence," she said, "but I got a letter from my uncle this morning—yes, here we are!—and he mentioned that an old gamekeeper I used to be rather fond of had died during the past few days." She turned the pages, looking for the paragraph in question. "He had a heart attack, it seems ..."

"Where was your uncle writing from?" Steed asked.

Emma looked at him. "The shooting box at Birningham," she said softly. "About five miles from the Wash."

Steed bent down abruptly and scooped up the newspapers. "I did ask you to drop in for an aperitif before lunch, my dear," he said. "In the circumstances, I feel something more substantial is called for, perhaps! There's a new Colombian blend from that chap in Duke Street by the grinder. John Jameson in the cupboard. Cream on the doorstep. D'you think you could possibly cope with an Irish coffee while I make a call ...?"

While Emma busied herself with Moulinex and Cona machine, he dumped the papers on the rosewood desk, settled himself in a chair and drew the telephone towards him. First he dialled a number in three groups of three. The line was opened instantly, though no word was spoken at the other end. Steed immediately gave another number verbally—a number so secret that less than thirty people in the whole country knew it. There was a decisive click on the line, then the normal ringing tone. After three double burrs, a receiver was lifted and a man's voice said crisply:

"Control."

"Steed here," the undercover man said.

"Identification?"

"Played Portia in prep school *Merchant of Venice* in 1935. Three tries against Harrow Colts in 1937. Stroked the Head of the River boat in 1939."

"Go ahead, Steed. Thought you were resting."

"So did I. Something may have come up, though. Can you get L.7 at the Yard to do a spot check on area mortalities within the half hour—Grade One, three-day limit, computed against the Mean?"

"Of course, if it's necessary. What's on your mind?"

"I think it may be." Steed picked up the newspapers and read from them in turn. "Vanessa Arco, painter, 27, obituary in today's *Gazette*. Oliver Freesing, town councillor and prospective parliamentary candidate, 54, death mentioned in *Lincoln Mercury* announcement of change of speakers at political meeting tonight. Henry Atherley, doctor, 61, death in motor accident reported in today's *East Anglian Echo*. Got those?"

"Right."

"In addition, two more so far unreported: a gamekeeper at a village called Birningham a day or so ago; and a diner at a pub called the 'Ely Cathedral'—that's between Boston and Little Hornham—last night."

"Right, Steed. And the area?"

The undercover man picked up a large-scale atlas of the British Isles and read off a series of six-figure co-ordinates. "That should be wide enough for them to give a definitive figure," he said, "I'm at home. I'll expect your call in about half an hour, then?"

"In *exactly* thirty minutes," the impersonal voice said precisely.

The Napoleonic barrel clock on the desk was striking the half hour after eleven o'clock as Steed replaced the receiver on its cradle.

Soon afterwards, he was sitting cross-legged on his tiger-skin rug, the newspapers once again spread around him, as Emma spiralled the thick, slow cream over the back of a spoon on to the surface of the aromatic, whisky-laced coffee roasting in the steaming cups.

"You really think there's something here, don't you, Steed?" she asked as she curled up on the striped settee with her own cup and saucer in one hand.

"M'mmmm. Delicious, Mrs Peel. Delicious! Yes—I've been convinced of it for years. One of the most invigorating drinks—"

"Steed!" Emma cried warningly.

"But I have, my dear. One shouldn't be chauvinistic about these things, you know. Of all the arts, gastronomy is the most cosmopolitan. Because the Whisky is Irish, the recipe French and the coffee South American, that's no reason at all to deny the excellence—"

"Steed! I was speaking of heart failure, as you know very well."

"And so was I, Mrs Peel! As I was saying, this splendid drink is a first-class stimulant—but you're leading me astray, talking about food! If I may venture to change the subject, I'd like to get back to this affair of the deaths in East Anglia..."

Emma burst out laughing. "You really are incorrigible," she said. "Why *do* you do it?"

"Another kind of stimulation—using the female variety of logic *on* a lady," Steed grinned softly, rising to his feet and putting the empty cup and saucer on his desk. "Besides, the pink spots on your cheeks when you're angry are most becoming. Seriously, though—"

"*I* know," Emma interrupted again. "I'm doing a grand job. What I cannot see at the moment, is just where a job comes in to this at all. If you're right, that is, and there *is* something odd about these deaths... Unless"—she paused and eyed Steed suspiciously—"Unless you've known all along and are simply pretending to discover it stage by stage for my benefit. I wouldn't put it past you!"

Steed was contrite. "My dear Mrs Peel," he assured her, "you have my word on it that there's nothing going on—nothing at all—which you don't know as much about as I do."

"You're just playing an outsize hunch, then?"

"If you like to put it that way. You saw that man collapse last night. I wasn't entirely happy about the local GP's diagnosis. There were one or two things... But never mind. The point is that I happened to see these three newspaper reports this morning. And then you mentioned your father's letter—and the five deaths together suddenly seemed an awful lot to have occurred in the same way, in such a short space of time, in almost the same area."

"And so?"

"And so I've asked for a check. Just in case. At this moment, the girls in L.7, Scotland Yard's new liaison department, are doing a top priority run-down for me—correlating all deaths bearing any resemblance to these in a given area, during the past few days, and checking them against the national average."

"Of deaths from the same causes over the same period of time?"

"Exactly. I mean, see what we have already." Steed ticked them off on the fingers of his right hand. "One, a middle-aged man falls dead in the middle of a meal. Cause of death diagnosed as a heart attack. Two, an elderly doctor drives his car head-on into a horse trough. He is thought to have died of a heart attack before the actual crash. Three, an unconventional young woman, well known as a painter of birds—"

"Of course!" Emma exclaimed suddenly. "Birds! Vanessa Arco. She's the painter all the smart gossip columnists call The Beaknik!"

"That's the one," Steed smiled. "The Beaknik. She dies in an isolated studio—from a heart attack. And then there's your gamekeeper to make four, and the gentleman who never did make his speech at the political meeting coming in at number five . . ."

"And they're both heart cases too?"

"It seems like it. I know it could be coincidence, of course. But suppose it isn't—what on earth have all these people in common? Why should everyone suddenly start dying from heart failure in a corner of East Anglia?"

"But Steed, people die from heart failure all over the place, all the time . . ."

"Of course they do, my dear. It's just—how shall I say?— the . . . the *concentration* of it that seems a little odd to me in this case."

The barrel clock on the desk was striking twelve. Before it had got half way through its silvery pronouncement, the strident bell of the telephone was shrilling it into oblivion. Steed scooped up the receiver.

"Steed here."

"Identification; for mercy's sake."

"The quality of it's not strained. When you're at school, it droppeth like the gentle rain from heaven, upon—"

"All right, all right, all right. No need to show off, Steed. Some of us were on the science side. I have the gen you want."

"Splendid. Fire away."

"Within the coordinate and time limits, L.7 report nine deaths of this kind, including those you mentioned."

"*Nine?*"

"Nine. The plus percentage over the Mean is sixty-two. Six two."

"Thank you very much," Steed said. "Do you have details of the other four?"

"Of course. You have pencil and paper ready?"

"Of course."

But the undercover man did not write anything down as the voice dispassionately continued its report. He drew nine little men with glasses on the back of one of the newspapers, added moustaches to eight of them and breasts to the ninth, and finally doodled in what looked like a child's version of a seagull above the head of each. Eventually the voice stopped.

"Fine," Steed said. "Thanks very much again. Yes . . . yes, I see what you mean. *Quod erat demonstrandum,* as you chaps on the science side would have said . . ."

He put down the phone and turned to Emma Peel.

"In the last three days," he said, "nine people have died from unexplained heart failure in the neighbourhood we were in last night. Per hundred of the population, that's sixty-two per cent up on the national average for the same three days. And in six of the cases there was no history of cardiac trouble whatever."

In her turn, Emma whistled. "You *are* on to something, then, aren't you?" she asked.

"I'm afraid it does look like it."

"What about the previous figures for the area, though?" the girl pursued. "Perhaps there's a history of higher-than-usual cardiac failures for some reason."

"They were intelligent enough to check that, actually. Until these three days, it was dead normal, right on the average—for as far back as they were able to go in a half hour, that is."

"Then obviously you must be right—there's something . . . well, *wrong* about these deaths. We know about five of them; what did you find out about the other four?"

"A retired admiral dropped dead in his rose garden; a railway porter shuffled off this mortal coil between the 8.45 and the 9.15; a tramp was found stiff in a camp fire but wasn't burned; a 25-year-old insurance agent perished in his bed."

"And the places—the venues, as they say in show business?"

"Bratby, Little Hornham station, the roadside between Bratby and Flint's Dyke, and Boston," Steed said. He picked up the atlas from the desk again and opened it at the page showing the area they were discussing. "Let's mark in the nine fatal spots," he added. "Here, you take this red thing and ring the places as I call them out . . ."

"Well, I'll start with the Martello tower at Star Point," Emma said, making a neat circle on the printed page. "That's the furthest North. Then I'll do my gamekeeper at Birningham. That's the furthest South."

"Right," Steed said. "Then there's this long bit of straight road following the coast in between. That's where they found the tramp." He leaned over Emma's shoulder and indicated a spot on the map. "And a couple of circles at Bratby, a few miles further on. Those are for the doctor and the retired admiral. One at our pub, of course—that's ten miles or so inland and to the Northwest. And . . . let me see . . ."

"The Hornhams?" Emma prompted.

"Yes, of course. One at Little and one at Great, for the porter and the councillor. How many do you have now?"

"Eight."

"Well, that just leaves the insurance agent at Boston. Now, how does it look?"

Together they bent over the atlas and studied the pattern of red circles. "Seems as obvious as a signpost," Emma said at last. "You can't very well miss it, can you?"

"Absolutely not. Apart from that one-off example at Boston, all the rest are within a ten-mile radius of Bratby—and the concentration seems heavier as we get nearer to that village. Bratby has to be, as it were, the epicentre of the operation . . . whatever the operation is."

"Yes, Steed—but *why*; why should people begin dying off like flies around some obscure hamlet in the Fen District? If we accept that the deaths are deliberate, we still come back to that. What could anybody gain—what possible connection could there be—between the deaths of five professional men, a gamekeeper, a tramp and a lady painter?"

"That, my dear," Steed said grimly, "is what we have to find out."

"What d'you mean—*us*? It may be nothing to do with you, let alone me. It may be entirely a police matter, some local vendetta, an M.I.5 affair or a Special Branch party to do with ... with—oh, drugs or black magic. Anything. There must be some common denominator that would give a pointer, the way the circles did on the map. Couldn't all the conceivable details be fed into a computer—?"

"I didn't say 'us'. I said 'we'," Steed corrected her drily. "And L.7 already *have* fed all the available data to a computer."

"Well?"

"Well, there *is* a common denominator—which is why I think we ought to be on our way to Bratby."

"For heaven's sake, Steed! Do I have to wait for next week's bumper issue before I get another thrilling instalment?"

Steed grinned suddenly. He reached for Emma's coat. "Mrs Peel," he said smoothly, "your culinary expertise entitles you to an immediate explanation. You shall have one at once."

"Steed! What on earth has my culinary—what do you mean?"

"The common denominator, my dear! The one linking factor. Like our friend at the 'Ely Cathedral', every single one of the other eight victims was eating—or had recently eaten—some kind of duck when he died ..."

5

"IT LOOKS LIKE ONE OF OURS"

STEED decided to motor up to Bratby alone and telephone Emma that evening when he had spied out the lay of the land a little. "I may want you to come up and lend a hand, one way or another," he said nonchalantly. "But I shall probably know about that tonight. Anyway, I'll let you know when I phone."

"Yes," Emma said. "There is one thing, though."

"Really, Mrs Peel? What is that?"

"I may decide not to come. I may not *want* to come. Even if I was asked properly instead of told."

"Nonsense, my dear," Steed said heartily. "A spot of the good old East Coast breeze'll do you the world of good. Blow all those cobwebs away!"

He handed her courteously into the low-slung, black and white Lotus Elan she had left outside the street door of his flat, and waved good-bye as the little car rocketed away down the mews with a crisp snarl of its exhaust. Then he opened the big double doors of his garage and went inside to operate the electric lock of the steel grille behind them which protected the Bentley. He had thrown an umbrella, a pair of bowler hats and a weekend case on to the back seat and was just raising the bonnet to flood the twin carburettors when there was the sound of tyres on the cobbles and a taxi rolled slowly to rest outside.

"Cab, sir?" a voice called persuasively. "Cab, Mr Steed?"

Steed didn't look up from the engine room of the Bentley. "I should have thought it was fairly obvious that I was just about to go out by car," he called back. "It does start, you know..."

"Not until after lunch, it doesn't," the voice said. "Not today."

The undercover man straightened up and sauntered towards the doors. "Just who the devil d'you think you're talking to," he began ... and then he paused, a slow smile spreading across his face. "Why it's Benson," he said. "Didn't recognise you at first, my dear fellow. What are *you* doing here?"

The seamed little man crouching inside his overcoat on the

driving seat of the cab winked with a kind of reprehensible familiarity. "You better hop in, cock," he said hoarsely. "You got a lunch date."

Steed sighed. "O God," he complained, "not with—?"

"That's it, mate. Hole in one, as I daresay your posh friends'd say. His Nibs wants to see you."

"For lunch, you say? Not at—?"

"Right again, Mr Steed! At the club. Come on, now—orders are to get you there at half past, and it's nearly that now..."

"Hang on a moment, Benson. You'll have to turn that thing round: this is a cul-de-sac. I'll just nip upstairs for a couple of bicarbonate tablets while you do it."

Later, as the taxi threaded its way through a traffic jam on the short journey to St. James's, Steed slid aside the partition window, sat sideways on the collapsible, backward-facing occasional seat, and questioned the driver further. Benson had been batman to the Very Important Personage at whose command Steed was lunching—and had continued to work for him after the war as a kind of personal aide and courier in the Service. There was a strange *rapport* between the two men and the select band of agents who came into contact with His Nibs frequently found that the tough little Cockney was able to give them guidance on the way that unpredictable mind was working. And since it pleased His Nibs's schoolboyish sense of the dramatic to send his mandatory invitations to "lunch at the club" via Benson, the consequent taxi-rides usually saw a lot of fast talking. ("Though if you ask me, old man," an Harrovian colleague of Steed's once said, "there's no such bloody thing as a leak from that quarter. Every crumb of info that chap drops is dropped because H.N. has told him to drop it, you can depend on it.")

"So how is the old boy, then?" Steed enquired offhandedly, as the cab squeezed between two converging buses in Cockspur Street and shuddered to a halt at the zebra crossing at the bottom of Haymarket.

"Perishing old women!" Benson exclaimed. "Think the whole of the traffic all over bleeding London comes to an automatic halt immediately their toe touches the ruddy zebra!—His Nibs? Doesn't complain, Mr Steed. Doesn't complain; though we're none of us getting any younger, are we?"

"No," Steed said. "It's just that some of us are able to bear it more gracefully than others. You've no idea why he wants to see me, then?"

"IT LOOKS LIKE ONE OF OURS" 33

"Well, now, cock, I really couldn't say, could I? 'Xpect you'll find out when you're having your nosh-up with him. Talking of cock, though—and who isn't in this business!—I'd watch the poultry course, if I were you, cock..."

Steed sat back with a sigh of relief. This transparent piece of obliqueness was as direct a hint as he was likely to get that the summons was at least in connection with the same mystery that was occupying his own thoughts. Though how the old man had got on to it he couldn't imagine.

Benson edged the taxi into the swirl of traffic that was bifurcating round the island at the entrance to St. James' Street. "*I* don't know," he complained resignedly. "These perishing one-way streets! Gets more like driving in Rome every day..."

There was nothing Roman about the appointments of the club, however. That dismal building was notable only for the lack of imagination of its catering manager, and Steed and his host were able without any difficulty to find seats in splendid isolation at the end of one of the long tables in the funereal dining room.

"There we are, my boy," His Nibs said encouragingly. "Now what do we have today? Let's see... Why, look at that! *Pommes de terre Monte Carlo!* Would you believe it! D'you get it, Steed? ... Monte Carlo—gambling—*chips*... That's a fancy way of saying chips, you know. I call that jolly smart."

"Very droll, sir," Steed said dutifully.

"I think I'll have some. Doesn't do any harm to encourage these artistic fellers, what? And what about a spot of Lancashire hot-pot? I must say I like something substantial at luncheon. Feeds the inner man. D'you fancy some yourself, Steed?"

"Er—no. I think I'll... I'm not really very hungry, sir, actually. Perhaps I could just have some bread and cheese?" Steed said hollowly.

"Nonsense, my boy. You need something filling under your belt. You people are supposed to keep in tip-top condition, you know. I'll order you some hot-pot too. Now what shall we drink? You like wine, don't you?"

The undercover man admitted faintly to this sybaritic taste.

"Thought so. Somebody told me you're quite an expert on wine."

"Well, I wouldn't go so far as to say—"

"Rubbish, rubbish. No need to be modest about it, Steed. I understand the carafe *rosé*'s very good value here..."

And later, after Steed had listened to two golfing stories and a scabrous anecdote about a former head of Naval Intelligence, His Nibs shot a curiously penetrating glance at him from below the shaggy eyebrows and rapped out: "Now what's all this I hear about ducks?"

Steed told him. "I hope you don't think I'm trying to go into business on a freelance basis, sir," he added. "It was just that I wanted to be quite sure before I bothered you with it. I was going to drive up to Bratby this afternoon, as a matter of fact, to see what I could find out."

"That's all right, Steed. We encourage initiative, you know that. You did quite right. And I have an extra piece of information, I think, that will make your journey really necessary, as we used to say in the old days."

"I'm glad of that, sir. In a case like this, every little helps."

"What's that? Oh. Yes—well, I don't know if *you* know, but L.7 shoot me along a précis of any little query like yours that they get. Just in case it might interest me, you know. So does Control, for that matter."

"I didn't know, as a matter of fact, sir. I shall file the information away for possible use in the future."

His Nibs permitted himself a wintry smile. "No doubt. Well, it seemed to me that you might be on to something. So I told L.7 to keep on plugging—to take the thing as far back as they could before luncheon. They were able to continue your crosscheck for a six-month period and feed the data into their blasted computer before I left the office to come here. And d'you know what they turned up, Steed?"

"No, sir."

The old man across the table paused for effect, relishing the dramatic possibilities of what he was about to say. He popped a faintly sweating cube of Cheddar cheese into his mouth. "They told me," he said, munching stickily, "that apart from the nine deaths you know about, there had been in the past six months no less than seven other fatalities of the same nature in the same area."

Steed raised his eyebrows.

"Now I know that hardly raises the figure above the normal average," His Nibs continued before the undercover man could speak. "Unexplained and unexpected heart failures are common enough, God knows. But there was just this other point—all seven of 'em took place at the dining table. And as far as L.7

could tell, the majority at least were eating, or had eaten, some kind of bird!"

"Good Lord! I see what you mean, sir."

"Yes. So I think we can safely say there's a case to investigate."

"The only thing is," Steed said thoughtfully, "that the case—such as it now is—may just be a police matter. It may not (if you'll forgive the phrase) be our pigeon at all. At the moment, one just can't tell."

"I don't think you need worry about that, my boy. From all the indications, and I've been in this game a long time, you know, this definitely looks like one of ours... And if it turns out that I'm wrong—well, you can always hand over the dossier to MacCorquodale, can't you?"

"Yes, of course." Steed said. "Well, since I have your approval, I think I'll get ahead with it right away, sir."

"Splendid. But won't you stay for a coffee?"

"Well, no—er—no, I really feel I should be on my way, sir, thank you. It's—er—there's quite a way to go, you know. Thanks just the same."

"Just as you like. What are those two white tablets you're taking, though—you're not going to tell me you're on some blasted quack's diet, Steed? Don't think I haven't noticed you've been off your food today."

"No, no, sir. The only quacks connected with this case are the ducks. These are... these are—just a couple of throat tablets, you know. Been a bit dry around the mouth for the past few days..."

"H'mm. Go easy on them, young feller. I don't hold with chaps in your line of country taking to drugs," His Nibs said disapprovingly. "Nothing like a good meal to put you right if you're feelin' out of sorts. Best tonic in the world, I always say."

"I couldn't agree with you more," Steed murmured, thankfully making his exit...

6

THE CORPSE IN THE CARDBOARD COFFIN

At six o'clock on the morning of the third day the single pane of glass which served as the cottage's front window erupted inwards with a noise like a bomb bursting. Steed was awake and out of bed with a golf club in his hand almost before the last jagged fragment had shivered to the brick floor. A large, smooth stone with a piece of paper wrapped round it was lying on top of the rickety table.

He snapped off the elastic holding it in place and smoothed out the cheap paper. Two lines in crudely printed ballpoint capitals sprawled across the surface:

WE DONT LIKE MEDDLERS ROUND HERE.
GET OUT OF BRATBY—FAST!—IF YOU WANT TO STAY HELTHY . . .

Steed crossed the room in three strides and jerked open the door. A figure in dark trousers and windcheater—he couldn't tell if it was a man or a woman—was just disappearing over the crest of the huge storm-beach. He ran across the stretch of balding turf and ploughed up the sweep of shingle as fast as he could. But by the time he reached the top there was nobody to be seen. The quarter of a mile of reed-covered saltings between the ridge and Bratby village could have concealed an army. Smiling slightly, he turned with a shrug and retraced his steps to the cottage.

The village was nearly a half mile from the sea. From the high ground of Star Point to the North, a long spit of land ran southwards for several miles, separated from the mainland proper by a shallow lagoon which had silted up and become overgrown with marsh vegetation at its inner end. The cottage Steed had rented—it was only a shack, really, with a single room and a primitive bathroom and kitchen—lay on the seaward side of the storm-beach which formed the backbone of the peninsula and protected the saltings beyond it from all but the most severe gales.

Lower down, the lagoon boasted patches of open water before it ran out into the sea via the disused harbour at Flint's Dyke. But up here the reeds and grasses were pretty dense. It was possible to walk across the marsh from the cottage to Bratby, but only the wildfowlers knew the paths: the rest of the world went round by the head of the inlet.

For Steed, the position was ideal. It was early Spring still, and very few people troubled to walk up to the point and down the spit to the handful of fishermen's shanties scattered along its length. Apart from his own, so far as he could tell only one other shack was inhabited—a rambling structure of tarred boards about a mile to the South. And even this he had deduced from the nets drying on the stones, the upturned boat on the beach, rather than because he had actually seen anybody.

On the other hand although he was thus isolated, from the top of the shingle ridge he himself could mount a permanent and invisible watch on Bratby and its surroundings.

For the greater part of two days, he had been lying flat on the stones, scanning the old brick and weatherboard buildings of the village through powerful Zeiss binoculars. Behind him, the grey waves sucked at the shingle and the wind scoured the rolls of seaweed piled along the high-water mark. In front, across the rippling tufts of the marsh, the everyday life of the hamlet pursued its distant routine. A trickle of people visited the few shops in the High Street, farmers drove in from outlying areas and parked in the square by the church, the three pubs opened and closed. There was a certain amount of through traffic—cars, lorries, vans, an occasional army convoy, using the road from Lincoln which swung seawards beyond Flint's Dyke and followed the coastline to the South in the shelter of the storm-beach. But on his side of the lagoon, hardly a soul passed. A gang of schoolboys brawled down the water's edge one afternoon, throwing stones at the sea. Coasters steamed slowly across the choppy horizon. Once he trained the glasses on a group of men, far down the spit, who seemed to be launching a boat.

There was a rough track bordering the marsh on the inner slope of the ridge, and in the late afternoons he bumped the Bentley up to the point, past the Martello tower, and round to the village to buy food. Later, posing as a journalist writing a series of features on wild life, he drank at the pubs and tried to strike up an acquaintance with the locals. But this was wildfowling country; most of the men had to do with birds and were taciturn in the extreme. Until this morning, nothing had happened to jar the sleepy routine of the place.

Now, however, as Steed swept up the broken glass from the cottage floor, there was an expression of pleased anticipation on his rakish features: his ostentatious enquiries had born fruit. The word had got around and somebody, somewhere, had been stung to action.

Perhaps, now, things would begin to happen...

* * *

Thirty-six hours later, Emma Peel stood with three men in the angle between a high stone wall and a macrocarpa hedge. Darkness had fallen and fitful gusts of wind snatched at the flames of the oil lamps where they stood behind a makeshift sacking screen. Over the cemetery wall, crosses, stone angels and the sombre shape of an elm etched themselves against the sky in the reflected light of the torch Emma held shielded in one hand.

The Home Office pathologist was conferring in low tones with his colleague as the girl directed the man with the spade.

"Just about there, I should say— it won't be very deep," she said quietly.

The man thrust the shining edge of the tool into the ground, put one foot on the shoulder of the blade, rested his weight on it, and levered at the handle, grunting, as a great clod of the clayey soil broke loose from the surrounding earth. He shovelled it to one side, sank the spade in again, and dug away another. The ground immediately over the grave had been stamped flat and hard, but it had been a hurried job: once the compounded topsoil had been removed, the shovel sank in easily enough— though it was heavy work levering away the sticky clods. In a few minutes, he had dug away about eighteen inches and Emma laid a hand on his arm.

"Go easy," she said. "It can't be far now."

The man prodded experimentally with the tip of the spade and struck something hard. The two men and the girl leaned over the shallow hole as he scraped away, gradually exposing the box. Finally, he drove the spade into the mound of discarded earth and prised the coffin loose with his bare hands.

"Right," the pathologist said. "That's the first part over with. Let's get it to the mortuary and see what we can find..."

They put the box in the back of the plain, dark green Home

Office van and went back to tidy up. The man with the spade shovelled the earth back into the grave and patted it roughly down as the others rolled up the sacking screen, pulled up the stakes which had supported it, and doused the lamps. Despite the chill in the night air, there was a heavy dew of perspiration on his brow when he had finished. He wiped his forearm across his face, shouldered the spade and followed them back to the van.

"All right, Horrocks," the pathologist said briskly. "I'll take the shovel in the back with us. You know where to go: make it as quick as you can. I'd like to get back to Town before it's too late."

"Very good, Sir Charles," the man said. He climbed into the driver's seat, started the engine, and drove slowly down the narrow lane until they reached the main road. A signpost showed briefly as the beam from their headlamps swept past while they were turning North. *Little Hornham ½*; *Boston* 11, the black lettering spelled out on the arm pointing in their direction. Behind them, the white finger indicated *Great Hornham* 3¼.

It was almost half an hour before the van pulled up in a covered yard behind high double gates. "Come on in," the pathologist called. "We can leave the—er—formalities to Horrocks and the attendants. I must apologise for having to bring you so far," he went on, "but this was the nearest mortuary the Home Office could suggest with the necessary laboratory facilities."

He led the way to a small, square room, tiled from floor to ceiling, comprehensively equipped with bench, sinks, flasks and retorts, Bunsen burners, racks of test tubes, microscopes, and shelves of brightly coloured reagents in glass jars. "Here you are, Wickham," he said to his colleague. "It's not very large, but I imagine you'll find everything here that you need. You're the analyst, though—what *will* you need?"

George Wickham was tubby, red-faced and moustached. Beside the lean elegance and grey-haired distinction of Sir Charles, he looked rather like an old-fashioned music-hall comedian trying out a new straight man.

"Well—ah—thank you, Sir Charles," he said. "Microscopes and slides, of course. The usual culture dishes, I suppose. Spectroscope. Our normal—ah—apparatus for reaction tests . . . But really, this is a little beyond my experience. Perhaps Mrs—ah—Peel could give us a more succinct idea of what's required?"

"If by any chance I'm right," Emma said, "none of your normal tests would reveal anything. I suggest that, instead of following the customary routine and methodically eliminating the possibilities one by one, we just try straight off for this one particular reaction."

"Just as you like, Mrs Peel," the pathologist agreed.

"It doesn't react like the alkaloids, you see. It's neutral to all the usual reagents. But if you know what to look for and you do suspect it, the test's as simple as you like. If it's what I think it is, all you'll need are a couple of slides and a test tube with a Bunsen."

"I must say this is beyond *my* experience, too," Sir Charles said. "It's most fortunate that you studied in Brazil, Mrs Peel. Were you reading toxicology at Rio university?"

"No, I was at Bahia. And I was doing pure mathematics," Emma said with a smile. "But I had friends in the biology department—and it's an absorbing subject . . ."

A few minutes later, white-coated and rubber-gloved, they were grouped around the chill slab of the autopsy table. Behind them, grey steel drawers—each bearing in its seven-foot length some grisly souvenir of terror and disaster—penetrated the cold-storage section. At one side of the table, Emma waited by a trolley of gleaming instruments, ready to assist Sir Charles; at the other, the analyst stood prepared to take notes. The corpse itself, laid out now awaiting their attention, looked small and somehow ineffably pathetic in the hard glare of the overhead lights.

". . . no obvious signs of violence," the pathologist was saying. "The neck's not broken. There is no evidence of any wounds, by shooting or otherwise. We're ruling out natural causes—at least for the purpose of this investigation. So we might as well carry on with the organs. I take it you'll be requiring vascular sections, Wickham?"

"Ah—yes, please, Sir Charles."

"I'll give you auricular and ventricular tissue, a bit of lung section, some liver—and you'll have to put up with whatever I can manage on contents. The time factor, you know; and the quantities . . ." He shook his head and sighed. "Want any kidney, by the way?"

The analyst looked across at Emma, his eyebrows raised enquiringly.

She shook her head. "Wouldn't be any use," she said. "And I

don't think you need bother too much about those contents: if it shows at all, it'll be in the heart or lungs, I think."

The pathologist grunted. "Thank God for small mercies," he commented. "Kidneys'd be devilish difficult in a case of this kind." Abruptly he gave a short bark of laughter.

The other two looked up, startled.

"I was just thinkin'—devilled kidneys," Sir Charles explained. "Now—if you'd kindly pass me the smallest of scalpels, Mrs Peel..."

The blade plunged into the livid flesh. Emma watched, fascinated, at the miraculous dexterity of the dissection, marvelling at the delicacy of touch which laid aside layer after layer of skin, muscle, nerve and tissue until the required region was laid bare—and then wondering anew at the precision with which the exposed organ was itself stripped down.

A half hour passed. From time to time, Wickham went into the laboratory to prepare his slides and stain his specimens. The pages of his notebook became gradually filled with spidery notations.

A door to one side of the cold-storage drawers opened and a fat man in blue overalls came in carrying a trayfull of steaming cups. "Perishing cold in here tonight, I must say," he observed. "I thought you might be glad of a nice cup of tea."

Sir Charles looked up. "That's very thoughtful of you," he said warmly. "Very. I could do with something hot... Mrs Peel: another clip, if you please."

A few minutes later he laid down his scalpel and stood back. "There we are," he said, "that's it. The rest's up to Wickham and to you. Now for that tea..."

While they were waiting for the analyst to complete his preparations, he walked meditatively around the slab looking at the remains laid on it. "What I can't understand," he said conversationally, "is how the stuff—if it's there—can have got there. You say it's only fatal if it's ingested in the bloodstream or actually consumed?"

Emma nodded.

"Then how the devil did this chap get it—if he did?... I say! Wait a minute... Look at this!" He indicated a tiny scratch on the flesh. "There's a cyanosed discoloration around the abrasion. Now I wonder..."

He picked up a limp leg and flexed it experimentally. "Yes,

look!" he said excitedly. "That metal anklet he's wearing: it could have made that scratch. See—the sharp edge here fits exactly! We'd better have it off him and take it in to old Wickham..."

He hurried in to the laboratory, with Emma at his heels. The analyst was sitting on a high stool bending over a microscope. "All negative or neutral," he said, "just as you thought, Mrs Peel. There's just your special test to do, if you could give me the stuff."

Emma produced a small phial of oily, green liquid, poured a few drops into a test tube, took the tube in a pair of crucible tongs and heated it in the flame from a Bunsen burner, agitating the fluid gently until it boiled. She laid the tube in a wooden rack, extracted a small amount with a pipette, and allowed a single drop to fall on to a section of tissue on a prepared slide labelled "Lung".

"According to the Moraes test," she said, handing the slide to Wickham, "a drop of Herskovit's Reagent added to this will turn the cells violet if the reaction is positive."

"And if it's negative?"

"There'll be no change."

The analyst nodded, clamped the slide in position and adjusted the eyepiece of the microscope. He reached out to one of the shelves, took down a bottle half full of pale yellow liquid, and decanted a little into a clean test tube. Then, picking up another pipette, he closed his forefinger over the open end and transferred a drop to the slide. After a moment, he grunted and leaned back on his stool, allowing the others room to peer into the eyepiece.

The complex cellular structure of the tissue, stained a vivid green by the first fluid, swam in Emma's vision as the globule of reagent, vastly magnified, spread slowly across it. The cells blurred, became muddy—and then suddenly cleared, all at once springing into relief in a hard and brilliant purple.

"Positive, by Jove!" the pathologist breathed. "So you *were* right."

Emma smiled. "I'm afraid so," she said. "One of the world's most deadly poisons—a rare derivative of *Curare* that's odourless, tasteless, soluble in water, and virtually undetectable unless you know what to look for. We'd better have a look at the others, just to make sure."

The slides marked "Stomach contents" and "Liver" gave

negative reactions, but sections taken from both sides of the heart were positive.

"Well—ah—that definitely settles it," Wickham said. "The poison was not consumed but entered the bloodstream directly, where it would quickly produce syncope and total paralysis of the muscles of the lungs. Death would follow almost at once— either through stoppage of the heart's action or through—ah— asphyxia."

"We think we know how it got into the bloodstream, too," Sir Charles said. "I wonder would you mind doing one more, my dear fellow?" With infinite care, he scraped a spatula against the inner surface of the metal anklet they had brought through from the mortuary. A few tiny grains of a white-ish, crystalline substance detached themselves from the metal and fell on to the filter paper he had placed beneath. Wickham re-heated the test-tube carrying Emma's green liquid, shook the contents of the filter paper into it, placed the tube in the flame once more, and then dropped in half a c.c. of the reagent.

The hot fluid frothed and became opaque, turning gradually to a dirty rust colour. Then abruptly the whole length of the tube was translucent again—in the same bright, glittering purple.

Sir Charles nodded his head several times. "Just as I thought," he said. "The poison was on that metal thing, and he scratched himself with it."

As they walked through the mortuary on their way out, he stopped by the corpse on the slab. "Not a bad bit of flesh on him," he said, patting it familiarly. "In happier circumstances, I wouldn't have minded sinking my teeth into that bird—provided he'd been roast, of course."

"It's just as well you didn't, Sir Charles," Emma said with a grim smile. "Who would there have been to have done the P.M. on *you*?"

She picked up the remains of the dead duck from the slab and shovelled them back into the shoe-box in which it had been buried.

7

ENTER A GIRL WITH A SHOTGUN!

"WHAT I cannot understand, Steed"—Emma Peel said—"is how you knew the duck would be there. I mean, what on earth made you think we'd find the body of a poisoned bird buried outside Little Hornham churchyard? And where did it come from?"

"It came from the 'Ely Cathedral'," the undercover man said. "It might even have been the one we were going to eat, for all I know. And there's really no mystery about how I knew where it was: Lurchman told me."

"But I still don't see—"

"I didn't think they were actually responsible for the man's death—at least not directly. But I knew there was something odd going on in that pub, so I drove across to see Mark the night before last and—er—put the screws on a bit," Steed said.

They were sitting on the shingle outside the rented cottage, lobbing pebbles at a tin floating a few yards offshore. The wind had dropped for once and the sea was calm. In another half hour, the sun would have set, but now there was still a faint warmth in the Spring afternoon.

"What did you find out from our late host, then?" Emma asked, scrambling to her feet to dust off the black leather trousers she wore beneath a severe overblouse in white twill.

"Well, he was very reluctant to tell me anything at all—kept on being evasive, saying he couldn't see what I was getting at, and so forth. But then I sort of—well, pointed out how suspicious it would look if ever the police did decide to investigate, or if the doctor wouldn't give a certificate, or if there was an exhumation. And finally he decided to come clean."

"Did you tell him you'd seen him hand that package over to the girl when you were looking out of the bedroom window?"

"Yes—that was the ace up my sleeve. After that, he began to talk."

"I suppose the dead duck was in the package?"

ENTER A GIRL WITH A SHOTGUN! 45

"And you're quite right; *ab*solutely *cor*rect," Steed said in mock fairground barker style. "Give the lady in leather pants a cigar . . ." He picked up a fistful of small stones and began to hurl them one after the other at the tin. "The whole point is—*Splash!*—that Mark has a tremendous reputation to keep up. Any breath of scandal—*Splash!*—attaching in any way to his food, or the way he gets it—*Splash!*—could ruin his business overnight. And it appears that the ducks he was using last night were poached—*Splash!*—and not only that: there was, I think, something wrong with them. Perhaps they were found dead or something of that sort—*Splash!*—so at the first hint of any trouble he naturally got rid of them fast. That's why he was so shifty while we were there—*Splash!*—and why the ducks that had already been cooked had all mysteriously been thrown away."

Emma bent down and gathered a handful of stones herself, which she began to shy at the tin alternately with Steed's. "In that case," she said, "who was the girl—*Plop!*—and why did Mark give the parcel to her?—*Plop!*—Couldn't he just have buried the ducks—*Plop!*—himself?"

"He didn't want any part of it—*Splash!*—If there was anything wrong with the birds, they mustn't be associated with his precious kitchen—*Splash!*—So the obvious thing was to shoot them back to the poacher who supplied them and let *him* cope—*Splash!*—But so far as the lady was concerned, he wouldn't say a thing. Bit of a romantic interest there—*Splash!*—I fancy."

"Then his girlfriend—*Plop!*—was a kind of go-between, a contact linking Lurchman and the poacher?—*Plop!*"

"Exactly—*Splash!*—And in a few minutes we're going to set off to pay an unexpected visit—*Clang!*—to the poaching gentleman."

The tin sank, bubbling, beneath the surface.

"This is a silly game," Emma said, dropping the rest of her pebbles to the beach. "It's getting cold. I'm going to fetch a jacket."

"Don't be discouraged, my dear," Steed said. "After all, I used to be reckoned a pretty fair cover-point at school . . ."

Later, as they walked down the landward slope of the ridge to a boat he had somehow got hold of and concealed in the reeds, she made a thoughtful re-cap on what they found out so far. "It seems we have a bird—or birds—fitted with a metal anklet in some way carrying this poison," she said. "And that the anklet made a small wound when the bird scratched itself—which let the poison into its bloodstream and killed it."

"That's right," Steed said.

"And that the dead bird was found, perhaps with others, by a poacher, who sold it to the 'Ely Cathedral'."

"Exactly."

"And that the pub, furthermore, cooked one of these ducks in all good faith, as they say, and served it to the man we saw die?"

"Yes, my dear. But—"

"Well there are two questions, Steed," Emma interrupted, "that we haven't answered: was there any intention on someone's part to kill this particular man? And how was he killed anyway? The poison was in the *duck's* bloodstream—why did the man die through eating its flesh?"

Steed parted a six-foot clump of reeds fringing the marsh and handed her into a flat-bottomed Carvel dinghy hidden behind them. "Your second question's a matter of gastronomy," he smiled, taking up a long pole and nosing the small craft slowly out into the dense vegetation. "The sauce for *Duck à la Rouennaise*, as Mark told you, is made from red wine, onions, the liver *and the blood of the bird, which is collected by crushing the carcass in a special press* ..."

"Yes, of course," Emma said slowly. "And the poison doesn't break down or deteriorate either in storage or under heat."

"Quite. And so far as the mysterious guest is concerned, MacCorquodale has solved that one. Apparently he was a Lincoln solicitor, henpecked for years, whose wife—whom he loathed—had just died. And he couldn't resist celebrating ... though he was careful to do it incognito, in case any of his clients should think it lacking in respect!"

"Some celebration!" Emma said grimly.

In the fading light, the dinghy forced its way laboriously along the choked lagoon. Clouds of mosquitoes hung in the dank air, hovering like smoke in the gaps between tall reeds. Sometimes the channel widened to several yards, only to narrow again as the rushes closed in above their heads and the hummocks of rank marsh grass scraped along the gunwale. The sea was inaudible. The only sounds to break the monotonous plop and drip of Steed's pole were the furtive movements of night creatures hidden in the foliage and an occasional gurgle from beneath the boat. Several times he was forced to back out from a passage that became impenetrable and find an alternative route. Once something heavy splashed into the water from a floating island and swam stealthily away into the dusk.

"If, as you say, this poacher lives further down the spit," Emma complained in a low voice, "why on earth couldn't we have walked?"

"On that shingle," Steed replied, "you can hear someone coming half a mile off. I want to make sure our friend's there—so I prefer to drop in unannounced. And talking of camouflage, my dear, your protective colouring's almost perfect!"

Emma shivered and wrapped her thigh-length snakeskin jacket more tightly around her. "Some of our problems solve themselves as we go along," she said quietly. "But the most important one remains: how does this poison get *on* the birds' anklets? And who puts it there, for Heaven's sake, and why?"

"The anklets are the normal rings put on migratory birds so that they can be identified and a check kept on their movements—"

"Yes, Steed, I know, I know. But the poison—that stuff's dynamite! It's a hundred times more virulent than Curare itself. And it's soluble in water. If one of those ducks had survived and landed on water that was going to be drunk—on a reservoir, say—why, the implications are terrifying..."

"I know," Steed said soberly. "There's something exceedingly malevolent going on around here. It's up to us to track it down —quickly."

"I mean we don't even know how many deaths have been caused already. *Are* all nine of the people you heard about poison victims, by the way?"

"We don't know for certain. Sir Charles checked on the solicitor, just to make sure, and of course *he* is. H.N. got exhumation orders on the Martello tower girl, the doctor, the tramp and the others. We should hear the results of the P.M.'s tomorrow. And they may dig up *one* of the earlier seven, as a sort of spot check. But I should think it's a hundred per cent a foregone conclusion."

"Yes, but if you're right, how did *they* get poisoned? They weren't all eating at the 'Ely Cathedral'."

"I hope we may know more about that after we've asked a few questions *chez* Monsieur Poacher," Steed said, motioning Emma suddenly to silence.

The reeds parted and the dinghy glided out on to a stretch of open water several hundred yards across. He gave half a dozen strong thrusts with the pole and then crouched down in the stern with the girl, allowing the boat to drift noiselessly onwards.

To their left, the shingle ridge humped blackly against the sky. Across to the right, they could dimly make out an irregular line of bushes marking the mainland boundary of the lagoon. Gradually losing way, the Carvel approached the southern end of the open space, its passage opening an ebony wake in the weed covering the surface. Just before the reeds closed in again, Steed took a paddle and dipped it twice deftly in the water to bring the dinghy to the bank on the seaward side. He jumped lightly ashore and hitched the painter to a rotting tree stump half buried in the marshy ground.

"Come on," he whispered, holding out his hand for Emma, "the place is just over the ridge." He gestured vaguely towards the long, low outline of a roof barely discernible beyond the slope.

They had gone perhaps a dozen yards when the voice spoke from behind and to the right.

"Put up your hands and turn slowly around," it said. "And don't try anything funny—there's *two* barrels to this gun . . ."

Arms obediently raised, Steed and Emma swung back to face the lake. Thigh-deep in the dark water, she stood over against the reeds—a commanding figure in rubber hip-waders and a gleaming oilskin blouse. The long-barrelled twelve-bore was rock-steady in her hands.

It was the girl in the rain whom Steed had seen from the bedroom window at the "Ely Cathedral".

8

CONVERSATION WITH A POACHER

JIM REEVES was a gnarled little man with a nutcracker face and silver hair. He was sitting at a plain table squinting down the barrel of a shotgun when the girl kicked open the door of the shack and motioned Steed and Emma in with the twelve-bore.

"I found these two snooping about at the back, Pa," she said. Her voice was low and throaty, a disturbing trailer for the programme of soft intimacies which might lie concealed within the stiff confines of oilskin and waders.

Reeves put the gun down on the table, picked up a four-ten, broke it, and held the barrels up to the single electric bulb which lit the room. "All right Bella," he said, peering through each in turn, "bring 'em over into the light and let's have a look at 'em." One handed, he clapped a piece of four-by-two cotton waste across the neck of a small bottle of oil, inverted it to moisten the material, and then began to thread this through one end of a length of weighted wire.

"What's the weight of a pull-through?" Steed rapped unexpectedly as the girl shepherded them to the far side of the crudely furnished room.

"The piece of lead on the other end—" the poacher replied automatically, in a conditioned reflex to the old army tag. He broke off and looked up at Steed. A corner of his clamped-down mouth twitched briefly as he rose to his feet, the gun still in his hand. He was wearing faded blue trousers tucked in to gumboots and an old tweed jacket with huge patch pockets. Steed had no doubt that there were others, supported by shoulder straps, inside. From the brim of the battered trilby on his head, part of the greasy black ribbon dangled rakishly.

"Seems like you could be a sight too smart altogether, mister," he said mildly. "We're simple folk around here; we keep ourselves to ourselves. But we don't go too strong on strangers—and trespassin' can be downright dangerous, can't it, Bella?"

The girl's sullen face was hostile. Over the high storm collar of her oilskin, her dark eyes regarded Emma and Steed unwaveringly. "There's accidents happen sometimes," she said levelly. "A party shoots at a bird, say, and there's people behind the reeds that didn't have no right to be there. It's nobody's fault—but they're dead just the same."

"Wouldn't it be easier to shoot just the bird—and then give it to them to eat?" Steed drawled.

The girl's eyes blazed. "You've no call to say that," she cried hotly. "Mark didn't know a thing about—" She stopped abruptly in mid-sentence, realising what she was saying.

Steed laughed. "Believe me, Miss Reeves," he needled, "you don't have to kill anybody else if it's a murder charge you're looking for!"

"At the very least an accessory after the fact—and we're by no means the only people to know it," Emma added, piling on the advantage.

"Shut up!" Bella Reeves shouted. Her knuckles whitened on the stock and barrels of the twelve-bore, and the highlights across the breast of the tightly belted oilskin rose and fell agitatedly. "I didn't even *know* the man was murdered. Nor does Mar—Mr Lurchman. Who d'you think you are, skulking about behind people's homes, making accusations—"

"Stow it, Bella!" The poacher's voice was suddenly commanding. He lowered the weighted end of the wire through one of the barrels of his gun and then, shifting his grip, twisted it twice around an index finger and pulled the oil-soaked rag on the other end steadily through. "Now," he went on in a quieter voice, "I think we're due for an explanation, mister; and we aim to get one..."

Emma and Steed were standing—still with their hands raised above their heads—backed up against one of the room's board walls. Behind and to each side of them, a collection of antique guns was displayed on nails driven into the wood. An old fowling piece immediately behind him, Steed had noticed as they came in, was supported at two points only—through the trigger guard and under the long barrel. Throughout the exchange with Bella, he had been imperceptibly allowing his left arm to fall back towards the wall. Now as the back of his hand brushed the breech of the old gun, he inched it sideways until the knuckles touched the head of the nail projecting through the trigger guard. Stealthily, he separated the middle and index fingers and then closed them again over the nail, gripping the head between the lower joints. It was quite loose.

"Certainly you can have an explanation, Mr Reeves," he said easily, working at the nail with his knuckles. "There was no intention to offend, you know. I'm staying at the old cottage up at the other end of the spit, and I thought I'd show Mrs Peel here something of the wild life on the marsh, that's all."

"What's that got to do with threats about murder charges?" the old man asked gruffly. He began to feed the pull-through into the second barrel of the four-ten.

"Nothing, really," the undercover man said. Without moving his raised arm, he jerked his hand forward from the wrist, keeping the fingers pressed tightly together. Between them, the nail pulled out from the wall.

The fowling piece crashed to the floor.

As Bella Reeves and her father looked up, startled, Emma shot into action like an uncoiled spring. In one lithe bound she was at the table, seizing the edges in her hands and somersaulting across it in a forward roll. She came hurtling feet first off the far side before the girl had recovered from her astonishment, knocking up the barrel of the shotgun and wrapping her legs around Bella's waist in a scissors grip. One barrel of the twelve-bore discharged deafeningly, bringing down a shower of plaster from the ceiling, as they hit the boards together.

Before the poacher had time to reach for the gun on the table, Emma was on her feet again, the twelve-bore in her hands. "All right," she panted, "there's still one up the spout! Now—over there, the two of you, if you please . . ."

Bella Reeves got slowly to her feet, circled Emma warily, and joined her father over by the curtained window. Water, still beaded on the calves of her waders, slid down the heavy black rubber to leave a trail of damp footprints on the floor.

Steed hadn't moved. An elegant figure in charcoal trousers and a honey-coloured suede windbreaker with an olive green square at the neck, he was leaning against the wall with one ankle crossed over the other. Now he moved languidly over to Emma and took the gun. "Thank you, my dear," he said quietly. "That was most impressive . . . Mr Reeves, I assure you again that we didn't come here looking for trouble. We were in fact on our way up to knock on your door when your daughter—er—surprised us. We only wanted to talk to you for a moment."

"What do you want with me?" the old man asked suspiciously.

"I told you: to talk. And as a proof of our good faith"—he broke open the shotgun and extracted the spent and the unused cartridge—"I shall put this thing down for a start. You can't have a conversation over a gun, can you?"

He laid the gun on the table, picked up the four-ten and placed that beside it, and then collected the oil bottle, the pull-through and a handful of shells which had been scattered on the floor by Emma's exertions. "Now," he said, pulling up a kitchen chair, swinging one leg over it and seating himself astride with his arms resting on the back, "perhaps we can make ourselves comfortable for a few minutes?"

Reeves tried not to be impressed. He glanced from Steed to Emma and then back to the undercover man again. He moved unwillingly forward, tugging at his lower lip. "I don't know as I want to talk," he said reluctantly. "Anyway, it depends what you want to say."

"Don't talk to them, Pa," Bella said urgently. "No good'll come of it. They're only here to make trouble. You don't have to say a word."

The poacher absentmindedly retrieved the fowling piece from behind Steed's chair, accepted the nail from the agent's hand, and pressed it back into its hole in the wall, replacing the gun in its old position. "Now hold hard, child," he said, stepping back to scrutinise the effect. "No harm ever came just from talkin'. Maybe we ought to see what the gentleman has to say." He adjusted the position of the firearm fractionally and then sat down himself.

"You're perfectly right, Miss Reeves," Steed said reasonably. "Neither you nor your father have to say anything at all. But at least let me say what *I* have to say, and then you can answer or not as you please. But why don't you get out of those wet things —you'll catch your death?"

The girl glared at him for a second, and then sullenly began to strip off the waders and her oilskin. She was wearing jeans and a loose fisherman's sweater, beneath which her nubile young body moved easily. Emma hitched one slender hip on to the table and sat there, swinging a leg, as Steed spoke.

"I'll put it as briefly as I can," he said. "I'm not interested in how you make your living; it doesn't concern me in the least.

CONVERSATION WITH A POACHER 53

You're a wildfowler, let us say, and among other commissions you supply certain people around here with game; right?"

"Pa!"—it was Bella Reeves speaking—"Don't answer, *Please*."

"And if it's any help, Miss Reeves, I can tell you that in fact no breath of suspicion attaches to the landlord of the 'Ely Cathedral'. We know all we want to know about that affair. It's the others that interest us now."

Bella scowled. She jerked back the flimsy curtains and stood, arms folded, with her back to them, staring across the beach at the dark sea.

"What's it to you, anyway, mister?" the old man said. "Why should I tell you anything about my affairs?" He got up and began to pace nervously back and forth.

"For this reason," Steed said—and then, in a creditable imitation of a sergeant-major's parade ground voice: "That man . . . Att-en-*shun!*"

Reeves's limbs acted independently of the man himself. Before he realised what he was doing, the fingers straightened and the hands snapped back to a position just behind the trouser seams; the heels slammed together—and for an instant he stood ramrod stiff . . . then relaxed with a sheepish smile. "That's the second time," he said accusingly.

"Third time lucky!" Steed said lazily. "How long were you in the army, Reeves?"

"Twenty-five years, sir." There was pride in the man's voice.

"Whose lot were you with?"

"Eighth Army, sir. From Alamein on. With Colonel Trottson's unit."

"Parry Trottson? I saw him a couple of months ago, on leave from India. He's mapping the Himalayan foothills for the government, you know."

"Is he really, sir? He always was a one for the hard life. How is the old—how is the Colonel?"

"Blooming, Reeves. Blooming . . . If you were with the Colonel in North Africa, you must have been one of the Special Scouts—sabotaging Rommel's tanks, and all that?"

"That's right, sir. Fair old caper that was, and all."

"Yes, it must have been. I worked with Colonel Trottson myself, a little bit after that. In northern Italy, it was."

"Not with them eye-tie partisans in the Po marshes, kidnapping—"

"That's it, Reeves. But we don't talk about it now. The point is, I could do with an East Anglian partisan in these marshes here. Somebody's trying to set himself up as a sort of private Rommel, and it must be stopped."

There was respect tinged with admiration in the man's manner now. "You can count me in," he said. "What do you want me to do?"

"For the moment, wait until I call on you—but you can help a lot by answering these questions we were talking about."

"Pa, for the last time!" Bella Reeves burst out.

"Shut your mouth, girl. Why don't you do something useful instead of arguing all the time? Go get a broom and sweep up all that plaster from the floor there."

The girl flung out of the room with an angry toss of her head. After a glance at Steed, Emma followed. Soon, they heard the two voices—one furious, the other soothing and placatory—alternating from beyond the door.

"She's a good girl," the poacher continued, "but wild. Headstrong—that's what she is. Won't listen to reason. She was goin' on for a nurse, but she gave it up and come home to look after me when her Ma died three years ago. Not that she don't help me a lot in my work, mind . . . Still—what was it that you wanted to know, then?"

"Did you supply birds to many people around here?"

Reeves shifted from foot to foot. He looked embarrassed. "See here," he said. "I'm afraid I'll have to ask you to treat this as strictly confidential. The whole point of a connection like mine is the mutual *trust*—you know, *they* don't know you're poachin' 'em, and *you* don't know they're receivin', see?"

"I quite understand. You don't need to worry."

"Thank you, sir. Well, then—yes, I did. Most of the nobs."

"Doctor Atherley?"

"Oh, yes. Regular. He had something every week. And the old admiral—and David Oates at Hornham station. And the mayor. And the three pubs at Bratby. Oh, and that young lady up to the tower. Couldn't afford much, but she was nice . . ." He stopped, struck by a thought. "*Was* nice. I said it. And I just realised: half me clients are dead, aren't they. You don't think—?"

"I'm afraid I have to. D'you remember how many of these people bought birds you'd *found* dead—recently, that is?"

The poacher looked uncomfortable. "You understand, sir—

it's not the sort of thing I *usually* . . . I mean to say, I supply game; I go and shoot that game—or trap it or whatever. But in this case . . . well, it wasn't as if they'd died of some disease or other, or been killed by something else. Why, some of 'em were still *warm* when I found them! And it seemed a shame to waste them . . ."

"And you *do* remember?"

"Well, that's not to say—well, yes. Some of 'em. The mayor never. And the pubs never. But the bird at the tower, she had one. And so did the doctor and the admiral. Oh, and Lurchman, of course—he had several. As for the rest, I can't rightly tell. Difficult to sort 'em out, anyway, once they're in with those I got meself. There *were* others, though."

"They were all ducks, were they—the dead ones?"

"Couple of Teal. Rest were Mallard."

"Where did you find them, Reeves?"

"Ah, now, look, sir—you're asking me to give away the secrets of me trade. A free fowler—I don't hold with the word Poachin'—has to take his chances where he can get 'em. You wouldn't believe the number of busibodies, and gamekeepers, and enforcement officers, and police, and game laws you can run foul of up here. And then there's the nobs themselves—the mugs who *pay* for licences. What with this and that, a man keeps a good bit of territory to himself when he finds it."

"Remember Rommel, Reeves."

"Yes, sir. Well . . ." The man was obviously reluctant. ". . . Well, the most of 'em come from the old Mendip place, and that's the truth of it."

"The old Mendip place? Where is that?"

"It's a bit to the south'ard—mile or so beyond the Dyke."

"What is it, a farm?"

"Bless you, no. Bloody great red brick mansion, used to belong to old Sir Hugh Mendip when he was alive. It was built in his father's time, they say. Stands just off the coast road in about a hundred and fifty acres of saltings."

"Who does it belong to now?"

"Couple of right nut cases, if you ask me. One of 'em is a professor; name of Charnley—muckin' about all day and night in a ruddy laboratory they've built. The other one—it's him the place really belongs to—is Sir Albert Charles Frobisher Warbeck-Simner, no less. Too bloody blah for words! He's supposed to be an ornithol—orni—well, he's mad on birds, anyway."

"Ornithologist?"

"Yes, that's it. Well, he's got a bird museum there, and a whole zoo full of cages, with everything in 'em from a wren to an eagle. And the whole property, all of the marsh around the house, is a kind of bird sanctuary."

"And so you find it a very profitable—er—row to hoe?"

"Well, at least you don't get these idiots in plus-fours and moustaches banging off at everything in sight all day long! Got to be very careful, though: it's strictly night work, or just after dawn at the latest."

"Why do you say that?"

"They can see everything you do, otherwise. That's why. They got some kind of crazy camera in one of them turrets—at least, I think that's what it's called. And they see what goes on all over the saltings."

"Not a *camera obscura*, by any chance?"

"Yes. That's it. That's what it is."

"How delightfully *fin de siécle!* Shades of *The Eye In The Museum!* But you seem to be extremely well-informed about the place, Reeves."

The old man looked down. He coloured slightly. "Well, to tell the truth," he said, "my girl goes over there and does for the two old blokes. Bella's in service there, in a manner of speakin'."

"Biting the hand that feeds your daughter, eh?" Steed smiled. He got up and put the chair back against the wall. "We must go. I'll fetch Mrs Peel, if you'll permit me—and thanks for being so frank."

Jim Reeves thrust out his lower jaw and gnawed at his stubbly top lip. He appeared distressed. "Look, sir—all these people," he said: "I never *knew*; honest ... I mean, I admit I pay no mind to the game laws, but that kind of lawbreakin's one thing; sellin' folks poisoned food's another. I never dreamed there was anything wrong with those bloody birds. Otherwise I'd never for a moment—"

"Don't you worry, Reeves," Steed interrupted, clapping him on the shoulder. "Nobody blames you for their deaths. I'm sure you acted in good faith—it wasn't your fault."

"Yes, but the poor sods are dead just the same, aren't they?"

Steed was adjusting his silk square in a cracked mirror that was hanging beside the door. "Don't blame yourself. *Somebody's* responsible—and I'm going to find out who it is," he said grimly.

Emma was helping the poacher's daughter to gut a small pile of fish in a scullery at the end of a passage with two tiny bedrooms leading off it. Bella kept her back resolutely turned as Steed and her father came in. Beyond her, in a sort of lean-to porch, a row of dead birds in assorted shapes and sizes hung from a rail. Small-mesh nets were looped on pegs driven in to one wall, fishing rods leaned in a corner, and on the brick floor a pile of gins, traps and snares gleamed faintly in the light from the scullery.

Steed wandered out on to the porch. Three sleek cats were lapping milk from an enamel bowl on the floor. A retriever curled up in a basket below a long bench opened an eye to look at him and then went back to sleep. Cages piled three deep on the bench held live rabbits, pigeons and ducklings. The pigeons were obviously the subject of some veterinary experiment, for—like temperature charts in a hospital—pieces of paper bearing scrawled notes and dates were pinned to each cage, while the rows themselves were labelled "*Ailing*", "*Treating*" and "*Helthy*."

"Come, Mrs Peel," Steed called. "We must take our frail craft and steal softly away into the night . . . Goodnight, Miss Reeves. Thank you so much for having us." He unlatched the door leading out into the night, then paused, gesturing to the pigeon cages with their mis-spelled label. "Oh, and by the way," he added, "next time you want to send me a message—use one of these, would you? The East Anglian dawns get so cold with no glass in the windows . . ."

9

BELLA GOES TO WORK

BELLA REEVES'S one souvenir of life in the city was a Moulton bicycle. On four days a week, she collapsed this small-wheeled machine, ferried it across the marsh to the main road, tied up her boat, and then assembled the bicycle and rode South to the home of her employer. Turret House was several miles from Bratby: beyond Flint's Dyke and the end of the lagoon, past the long, straight stretch of road where the body of the tramp had been found, beyond the turning for Ely and the Hornhams —a good fifteen minutes ride.

Remote and isolated across the sweep of marshland, the building itself was half hidden in a grove of trees, only the four corner turrets and the central tower with its green copper cupola being visible from the road.

The girl arrived at five minutes to nine on the morning after Steed's visit. She dismounted by the massive brick gateposts flanking the drive and wheeled her bicycle towards the centre portion of the wrought iron gates. There was a small button inset in the metal. A second after she had pressed this, a sharp click presaged a crackling of static before a disembodied voice rasped:

"Who is it? What do you want, please?"

Bella leaned forward and spoke into the louvred steel box attached to the inner side of the gate. "It's Bella, Professor. Bella Reeves. It's my day today—alright to come in now?"

"Ah, Miss Reeves! Jolly good! You're very punctual, my dear; very. Yes—come up at once, do," the voice grated. "But be sure you pay attention to the old yellow line, what! It would never do if you were to actuate the alarm—cry havoc and let loose the dogs of war, eh?" The sentence ended in a little wheeze of laughter, followed by another loud click as the apparatus was cut off. An instant later there was a buzz from the mechanism controlling the lock, and Bella pushed open the gate and wheeled her machine inside.

Two hundred yards down the road, screened by the clump of

BELLA GOES TO WORK

bushes masking a lay-by, Emma Peel sat on the roof of her Lotus and watched. Like the tree-lined causeway leading across the marsh to Turret House, the main road, too, ran along the top of a dyke here—and from her vantage point, Emma could easily follow the girl's progress through Steed's glasses.

The causeway was dead straight, and for about two hundred and fifty yards of its length, Bella pedalled steadily towards the house. With that peculiar, high-geared, loping movement imparted by the bicycle's rubber suspension, she appeared and disappeared behind the boles of the plane trees with monotonous regularity. Then, curiously, as the drive ran for a few yards between a line of white painted posts linked by chain, she lifted her legs to the handlebars and coasted, before dropping her feet to the pedals once more and cycling out of sight round the corner of a shrubbery fronting the building. For a moment more, Emma scanned the gothic chimneys, the turrets, the mesh tops of aviaries among the trees, and the roofs of outbuildings which showed behind the house. She noted that there was a thin spiral of smoke rising from the most northerly stack; that the turret windows and the few dormers she could see were uncurtained; and that there was something bright catching the early morning sun from the summit of the copper dome. Then she slid to the ground, put away the glasses, insinuated herself into the driving seat and drove back to report to Steed.

Bella traversed the gravelled sweep in front of the great portico, turned down the side of the house past a balustraded terrace, and rode into the brick-paved yard at the back. Bounded on two sides by the L-shaped block of the old stables—which now housed an extensive ornithological museum—the yard gave directly on to the kitchen quarters of the house itself. A long, low ferro-concrete construction in which lay the professor's laboratory completed the rectangle. Further back, the aviaries dotted what had once been a walled garden before the ground dropped away to the marsh.

At the laboratory entrance, Charnley was waiting: a spare little man with thin, pursed lips drooping at the corners, a beaky nose, and small, bright eyes behind oblong spectacle frames.

"Good morning, good morning, good morning," he cried cheerfully as Bella dismounted. "I wonder would you mind helping me tidy up the lab a bit before you do anything else today? Sir Albert doesn't want his coffee until eleven."

Bella didn't like the laboratory. Partitioned off at one end was what looked very much like a miniature operating theatre, with a steel table, chromium trolleys carrying gas cylinders looped with sinister corrugated tubing, and a rack full of shining syringes. Usually, there were hutches or crates full of live creatures—rats, guinea pigs, birds, and sometimes rabbits. Once, when the professor had been in there behind locked doors, she had heard a rat screaming like a baby.

Today, however, Charnley only wanted her help with what she thought of privately as the clinical part of the place. The tiled benches and porcelain sinks had to be cleaned; there were dozens of test tubes, retorts, flasks and crucibles to be washed; slides and culture dishes to sterilise; and complicated apparatus to dismantle and store away.

The scientist kept up a sporadic flow of chatter as he directed her efforts. He had a mercurial temperament, alternating periods of elation—when his schoolboyish enthusiasm bubbled over in bursts of gossipy trivia—with moods of depression when the least remark was liable to make him boorish and tetchy. Bella found him difficult to get on with and would much have preferred to do the work alone.

"It's getting on, the great work's getting on famously," he prattled. "My investigations will be completed—should be completed, that is: you never can tell with research, my dear—they *ought* to be finished by the time Sir Albert is ready ... He's a very clever man, you know; a pioneer ... That's it: put that flask on that shelf along with the others ... He'll be jolly pleased, I can tell you ... Sir Albert's a splendid fellow, really splendid. But he does like things to work out on schedule ..."

"What's the great work going to be, then?" Bella asked idly, running the cold tap into a bell-jar misted over with an oily condensation.

"Oh ... you know. Scientific research, my dear," Charnley said evasively. "You wouldn't understand—but it's going to make both of us jolly famous, I can tell you. People to be reckoned with ... No. Don't touch that piece of apparatus: I haven't finished with it yet." He gestured towards an elaborate construction of distilling retorts and cooling towers of spiralled glass from which electrical leads snaked across the bench to a power plug on the wall. Bella reached out for a wide-necked flask nearby which appeared to be empty except for a mush of greyish crystals lining the bottom.

"*Leave that alone!*" the scientist snapped. "Really—why can't you *listen* and do what you're told? . . . Put it *back*, I say! Now wash your hands. At once . . . That's it. Thoroughly . . . You want to be careful, you know. If you handle some of these things and then put your fingers in your mouth, you could get—you could make yourself ill." He looked quite white with anger, and there was a beading of perspiration on his upper lip.

At eleven o'clock, the girl made coffee in the great, bare, old-fashioned kitchen and took a tray into the study.

Charnley was slumped in a leather armchair, gnawing at an empty pipe. Bella drew up a low table, put the tray on it, and spoke to Sir Albert Warbeck-Simner, who was sitting behind a flat-topped desk covered with papers and books. "Would you like to pour yourself, today, sir?" she asked. "Or would you prefer me to do it?"

The ornithologist looked up. He was a big man, six foot two and heavily built, with a great, domed head innocent of hair except for a feathery tuft over each ear. His features were coarse in the manner of an 18th century aristocrat, with thick lips and insolently drooped eyelids. And his voice was deep and surprisingly mellifluous. Paradoxically—as Bella had often thought—it was the ornithologist who looked as though he could be a scientist, and Charnley, with his dry, hurrying voice and birdlike appearance, who could well have been an expert on the feathered world!

Bella repeated her question, as Warbeck-Simner had not replied and was still looking vaguely in her direction.

"Eh? What's that? What did you say?" he asked suddenly.

"The coffee, Sir Albert . . ."

"Ah, yes. Pour it out yourself, Reeves. My word, but that smells good, doesn't it Charnley?"

"Delicious," the scientist said perfunctorily. "You were about to say, my dear Sir Albert, that in a few days . . ?"

"That in a few days the balloon should be ready to go up. I've not decided finally which species—but it doesn't do to have everything too cut and dried, does it?"

"Oh, by no means, by no means . . . Ah—*three* lumps today, I think, thank you, my dear."

"I mean to say, it would never do if Worthington and his men got to hear of it too soon, would it?"

"No, no. It would never do if Worthington and his men got to hear of it," Charnley repeated with a gusty chuckle. The two old men giggled together like a pair of schoolboys, stirring their coffee and glancing slyly at the girl.

"How are your experiments with the birds going?" she asked conversationally, as she picked up the tray and prepared to leave.

"Birds, birds? What do *you* know about birds? Why don't you mind your own business? Your place is in the kitchen—not asking impertinent questions of your betters." The scientist was on his feet, trembling with rage.

Bella backed away, startled by the vehemence of the outburst. "I'm sorry... I didn't know—I mean, I thought..."

"You are not employed to think, Reeves," the ornithologist said severely. "Really, I can't think what the servant classes are coming to..."

An electric bell shrilled warningly in the hall outside.

"... The gate," Warbeck-Simner said, breaking off his rebuke. "Go and see who it is, will you, Reeves?"

The girl turned and left the room. He stared pensively at the muscular movement of her haunches beneath the cheap cotton dress, at the twin bulges of taut flesh above and below the outline of her brassière strap. He sighed. "A comely creature," he said. "But a little too inquisitive, I fear. What did she mean about the birds? I trust you haven't been indiscreet, Charnley. I hope you haven't been talking out of turn to her. Because if you have..."

The Professor was pacing up and down in his agitation. "I, my dear chap? Most certainly not. Absolutely no. Really, I assure you... I suppose she must have a *certain* intelligence, after all. She sees the crates. She sees me working. *Experiments* is one of the few scientific words she knows—so I suppose, really, it's quite a natural, innocent question. It was perhaps foolish of me to become so upset."

"I suppose so," Warbeck-Simner mused. "I hope so. Because if it's... more than that—well, we shall have to... take steps."

Bella Reeves poked her head around the door. There was a sullen set to her full-lipped mouth and she still had a heightened colour. "It's the boy from Lorimer's with the fish," she said curtly.

"Very well," her employer said. "Tell him to leave it at the gate. Then go down and fetch it—and you can start some of the housework before you prepare it for luncheon."

They heard her speaking into the talk-back installation by the front door, relaying his instructions. Then, a few minutes later, she passed outside the window on her bicycle.

Meanwhile, Warbeck-Simner had crossed the room to the wall behind the door. Unlike the others—covered, apart from window embrasures, from floor to ceiling with books—this had a practical and mechanical air. At one side there was a complicated Ampex tape deck, vertically arranged with a dozen output channels, each boasting switches and rheostat controls. Next to this, amplifier, pre-amplifier and turntable of a high fidelity record-playing unit were neatly housed on tailored shelves. Discs and boxes of recorded tape were stacked on the far side, alongside a unit containing three separate television screens—one orthodox and two closed circuit. Twelve-inch speakers inclined downwards from the two top corners. And centrally placed, like an electronic desk jutting from the wall, was a console—a slanting surface crammed with dials and buttons and indicator lights from which all this apparatus could be controlled. Here were bass, treble, volume and filter controls for the hi-fi; three different sets of knobs for the televisions; an inset panel from which the Ampex could be worked; banks of warning bulbs in various colours, each labelled with coded letters and numerals—and a special raised deck marked *Camera*. This bore two switches—labelled *On/Off* and *Shutter*—and two wide knobs with milled edges. One was surrounded by a graduated scale calibrated in ten-degree units from zero to 360; the other was similar, but the pointer moved through an arc of only 45 degrees. They were marked respectively *Scan* and *Incline*.

The ornithologist had switched on one of the closed circuit televisions. As a picture assembled on the screen, he moved a pointer to a position marked F/G on the dial. The screen momentarily blacked out, then abruptly swam into focus. Wherever the concealed camera was, it showed from slightly above a close-up view of the main gates. A youth in an alpaca coat was staring through the tracery of wrought-iron towards the house. As they watched, he shrugged, put a package in a narrow space between two bars, tried the locked gates again, and then walked to a small delivery van, which he got into and drove away.

A moment later, Bella Reeves cycled into shot, dismounted, and reached for the package. Warbeck-Simner grunted, and moved the pointer to D/1. The picture changed to a ground-level shot of the drive about a hundred yards from the gates.

After a few seconds, the girl came into view on her return journey. The package was tucked under her arm.

The owner of Turret House clicked the knob once more. This time it stopped at position D/3—further up the drive, almost at the house now. Bella pedalled into shot, lifted her legs to the handlebars, steering carefully past the line of white posts, then cycled off-screen.

"Nothing wrong there, eh?" Charnley said. "Nothing wrong there."

"No—but it's better to be safe than sorry," Warbeck-Simner replied. He switched the circuit off and turned on the other set—a fixed view transmission relaying only what was appearing on the ground-glass observation screen of the *camera obscura* at the top of the central tower. Charnley moved over to operate the *Camera* panel.

He turned the switch to *On*, moved the *Shutter* control.

The dark screen became light as steel blinds rolled back from the mechanism five floors above them. Gradually, a picture of sun-dappled foliage emerged. The scientist twirled the two knobs complementarily, inclining the prisms downwards through five—ten—fifteen degrees until the ground at the foot of the trees was visible, then swivelling the whole apparatus in a wide arc to scan the property. Thus he was able, as it were, to pan from the avenue of trees bordering the causeway to the saltings—and then, by slightly lessening the angle of incline as he turned, to track out towards the dyke and the road running along it. Apart from clouds of birds rising and settling on the marsh, the only sign of life was the tradesman's van disappearing into a dip at the furthermost limit of the dyke.

"Really, I fear you are becoming *too* suspicious," Charnley chided. "Everything was in order, you see."

As he spoke, Bella Reeves's head and shoulders moved past the window outside as she returned from her expedition to the gates.

"This time, perhaps," Sir Albert was saying sombrely. "But you simply cannot trust the lower orders, old chap. I mean, look at that girl's rascally father, for instance: does the old fool really think I don't know he comes snooping around the saltings three times a week, stealing my birds at night? ... As it happens, it—er—suits our plans for various reasons. But the moral's there just the same."

"Oh, I agree, I agree," Charnley said in his repetitive way.

"Just look at this wretched country. An empire thrown away in twenty years; thrown away. The government in the hands of middle-class illiterates and woolly-minded liberals—and the ruling classes, who by rights ought to be holding the reins, taxed almost out of existence! It's nothing short of monstrous, Charnley."

"Monstrous," the Professor agreed, his glasses glinting angrily. "And the intelligent men, the thinkers, the men of vision . . . reduced to the position of paid lackeys, hirelings of the civil servants."

Warbeck-Simner smiled. "Still," he said, "it won't be long now. When the Plan goes into operation, we'll show 'em, won't we? I bet there'll be a few red faces in Whitehall on *that* day!"

"You bet! Wouldn't it be super if only we could be there, though? Wouldn't you love to look out of the window of your town flat and *see* them? Wouldn't you like to see the *papers*?"

"No, no. Our place is out there at the despatching end. We'll come into it later . . . We can leave the rest to Worthington and his men!"

"Yes. Yes, of course. We can leave it to Worthington!"

And the two men burst into another fit of giggles.

"Come," the ornithologist said at last, dabbing his eyes with a handkerchief, "I want your help on these beastly anklets; perhaps if we used an *alloy* it would turn more smoothly . . . And you haven't told me how your experiments on the concentration are going . . ."

Chuckling, they walked out of the study arm in arm and made their way to Warbeck-Simner's workshop, which was housed in a corner of the museum. In the study, the closed circuit television screen continued to relay the eddying of birds on the marsh, the passage of an occasional vehicle picked up by the *camera obscura* in the central tower.

Bella was doing the housework. Apart from the viewing room at the top of the tower, the upper stories of Turret House were all unused, only the bedrooms and bathrooms on the first floor, and the dining room, drawing room, study and servants' quarters at ground level being furnished. The décor of the sleeping quarters was heavy and ornate, and it was over an hour before she had finished vacuuming the old-fashioned carpets, making the beds and dusting the intricately carved pieces and numerous cases of stuffed birds with which the rooms were strewn. As she was shaking a duster from the landing window, the ornithologist and the Professor were crossing the yard below, deep in conversation, on their way from the museum to the aviaries.

"It's still a bit parky, despite the sun," Warbeck-Simner was saying. "Gosh, won't it be wizard when we can put the Plan into operation and enjoy a bit of real warmth!"

"Wonderful, wonderful," Charnley said. "I can't believe we're really almost ready to go! I keep worrying that something will turn up to stop us, you know."

"What could stop us? I hear there's some journalist fellow from London nosing about in Bratby looking for material on wildfowl migration—but he'll hardly come bothering *us*, I imagine. And even if he did, the Trusty Retainers would jolly soon send him packing with a flea in his ear," Sir Albert replied—his fifth form phraseology as always contrasting oddly with his mature voice.

"True, true," the scientist was chuckling as the two men passed out of earshot. "I think we can rely on the Retainers..."

Bella picked up the vacuum cleaner and carried it down the broad central staircase. There was just time to do the study before she cooked the fish and called the two old men in for their lunch.

She crossed the room to the power point behind the desk, glancing casually at the closed-circuit television as she passed. Bending down to thrust home the plug, suddenly she paused, straightened, and turned back to stare at the screen and the area of marsh it showed.

The road stretched emptily along the top of the dyke. Reeds and rushes stirred in a breeze, oscillating their shadows across the hummocks of grass. On the patches of open water, floating birds preened themselves in the midday sun. There was nothing else to see.

The girl shrugged her shoulders, a faint frown wrinkling her forehead. Funny, she thought, bending down once more; she must have been mistaken... But for an instant—in the split second during which her travelling eye had swept the screen—she could have sworn that a man with a bowler hat and an umbrella had been sliding down the bank of the dyke into the shelter of a clump of bushes!

10

THE HOUSE ON THE MARSH

"BOWLER hat, umbrella and dark suit?" Emma Peel had said. "To go crawling about a marsh in? At *night*?—You must be out of your mind!"

"On the contrary," Steed had replied urbanely. "Suppose I should be discovered by Sir Albert Whatsisname? It is after all the first call I'm paying—and I hear he's a stickler for the formalities. Did you know you had ended your second sentence with a preposition?"

"But, good grief—surely you can't be serious, Steed!"

"We Steeds rarely jest . . . except when it hurts. Besides—there are certain—er—advantages to this particular ensemble which must for the moment remain a closely guarded secret."

And with that, Emma had had to be content. Steed's exasperating flippancy often concealed an inflexibility of purpose which only appeared in retrospect, and she had long realised that when he appeared at his most facetious, he was as often as not deadly serious. Accordingly, she had let the subject drop and told him what she had been able to find out during her brief vigil on top of the Lotus.

"There's only one way to get to the house, unless you go through the marsh," she had said. "And that's along the causeway. There's a barbed wire fence as far as the saltings—probably tricked out with alarm wires. And the gates are iron, about ten feet high, and controlled by an electric lock—they operate with one of those talk-back things you get in blocks of flats. There's no back entrance: the marsh extends on either side of the place and sweeps round behind it as well."

"Is the marsh itself fenced off in any way?"

"No. It lies considerably below the level of the road—probably below sea level, too. It starts at the foot of the dyke on which the road is built."

"I see. Is the sea far away?"

"Just on the other side of the dyke. It's a sort of sea wall really. There's a few bushes, a dozen yards or so of sea pinks and moss and mud—and then the shingle."

"H'm. And you say this story about the whole place being under the scrutiny of a *camera obscura* is true?"

"It could be. So far as I could see. There are four ghastly turrets in the worst Scottish Baronial style—about 1840, I should say—and this central tower, complete with cupola. There was certainly something up there that moved and caught the sun like a heliograph. If it *is* what you think, then absolutely everything that moves on that marsh—and on most of the road and the causeway, too—could be seen from the house."

Steed had sighed. "They do make things difficult, don't they?" he had complained. "Did you manage to glean anything of interest during your tête-à-tête over the fish guts with our rustic beauty?"

"She's not a bad girl, really. We got quite friendly in the end."

"I know. Her father told me. It's just that she's—er—a trifle on the headstrong side. Especially when she has a twelve-bore in her claws."

"She's never seen anyone around the place but these two extraordinary old men. But apparently they keep mentioning somebody called Worthington. 'Worthington's men' are a frequent subject of conversation—oh, and their 'trusty retainers', whoever they may be."

"Perhaps they have strong-arm men deployed around the place at night. After all, Bella's only there during the daytime, four days a week. And they could easily keep hidden while she's there—especially if, as you think, the upper floors are unused. Perhaps they are very clever old men."

"They could, of course, simply be two innocent old gentlemen who happen to cherish their privacy—no strong-arm men, no camera, no nothing."

"No. These—if you will forgive the phrase—are our birds. I'm convinced of it. It has to be them. What I cannot figure out is *why*. Why should an ornithologist and a scientist shove poison pellets into the anklets of ringed birds? Why should they let them loose?—there have been far too many for it to have been accident, you know. Why should they use wildfowl, if not because the stuff is soluble and wildfowl will get it to the water?"

"Steed—surely you can't mean . . . You don't think the poison's *supposed* to be dissolved in the water? Deliberately? That if the ducks hadn't killed themselves . . . ?"

"That tramp hadn't been eating duck—but he did die of the same poison. I contacted Sir Charles while you were on watch this morning. The poor chap had hardly begun his meal—he'd prepared some fish over a fire—but he had brewed up some tea and drunk that. Where did he get the water?"

"The marsh! But how dreadful, Steed."

"How dread-full. Literally. If I'm right, patches of that marsh may be as deadly as neat hydrocyanic acid . . . As a rule only migratory birds are ringed in a sanctuary like this. Imagine the Lea valley in North London, my dear—if your aesthetics can stand it. Think of the Lea Bridge Road and the huge reservoirs off it. Think of the others between Chingford and Waltham Cross. Birds migrate to those stretches of water every year—you can predict their arrival almost to the day."

"But, Steed—"

"Imagine yourself secure in Scandinavia, or sunny Africa, or wherever they come from," the undercover man had continued remorselessly. "The day before the pretty creatures leave, you pop in the pellets, the birds fly to the reservoirs, they settle and paddle about—and when the population turns on the tap to make the cup that cheers but does not inebriate . . . Hey Presto! Instant death!"

"But why not just drop in the pellets yourself?"

"Safety, my dear. How can *you* have done it when you're hundreds of miles away in another country? In other words, the perpetrators must be presumed to have the intention of coming forward and profiting in some way from the deed. But again how? And *why*? . . . I wonder . . . I wonder if these two old men are in some way the dupes of some organisation?"

"The familiar neo-fascist group—hoping to profit by the ensuing chaos?"

"The neo-fascist group indeed. Except that I don't know of one at the moment. Still—the mysterious Mr Worthington and his myrmidons, to say nothing of those retainers—they have a sinister ring to me."

"What can we do then?"

"As I said, I'm going to pay a social call on Turret House," Steed had said. "And then we'll see what happens . . ."

Now, having dropped from the rear doors of the fishmonger's delivery van as the young driver, suitably bribed, had slowed down behind the shelter of an alder thicket, the undercover man was preparing to sit it out until darkness fell.

He had figured that, if the road *was* under constant observation, the van might be watched until it was out of sight—but that the scrutiny might conceivably relax after that. He had therefore waited an hour in the shade of the thicket, and then slid quickly down the bank to conceal himself in a clump of reeds, where he proposed to remain until nightfall.

It was a strange world on the fringe of the marsh. The tops of the reeds rustled in the breeze, but down at ground level, completely sheltered by the dyke, not a stalk, not a leaf moved. The sun was quite hot, the air stagnant and heavy—and the whole atmosphere somehow brooding and oppressive. Behind him, the yellowed blades of last year's grasses spiked stiffly up the flank of the dyke. In front, through a curtain of ochre stems, he could peer at a segment of the saltings—alternating bands of coarse grass and mudflat punctuated by stretches of shallow water through which deeper channels occasionally carved their way. Here and there, patches of alder, whins and other marsh scrub islanded the desolate scene. Far off to the West, a line of trees signalled the existence of dry land, but closer at hand there was only the promontory of Turret House and its environs to break the monotony. Except, of course, for the birds—and they were everywhere.

Great flocks of Mallard and Pintail speckled the dun flats, rode in colonies on the water, and continually took off or landed on apparently urgent errands. Nearer to Steed, a gaggle of Greylag geese nattered among themselves. There were Teal, Sheldrakes, Tufted Ducks, Crested Grebes, and a pair of large birds that Steed thought were Goosanders—while among the rushes and grass around him he identified Reed Warblers, Buntings and a Water Rail.

For a long time he sat cross-legged on the ground, taking evident pleasure in the teeming life of the sanctuary. But at last he glanced at his watch, sighed, and picked up his umbrella— one of many in his collection which was not what it seemed. First he unscrewed the handle, an unusually fat one in curved malacca, from the lower end of which he removed a small cork. Next, he took off the wide ferrule, extracting from inside it a tiny beaker of stainless steel. This he filled with cognac from the hollow handle. He drank, refilled, and drank again. And finally he dismantled the entire parasol part of the umbrella, including the ribs, leaving himself holding just the shaft. This was in fact a slender but powerful spyglass: all he had to do to make it operational was to reach into his pocket for a small lens, which he screwed to one end, and a wide eyepiece, which he attached to the other. Then, cautiously parting the reeds, he put the device to one eye and aimed it across the marsh at Turret House.

A pair of Coots, which had become accustomed to the strange visitor and were paddling about in the water just beyond the stems, bobbed away with shrill cries of alarm. And a black, white and chestnut duck with a bright scarlet bill waddled angrily down from the hummock where it had been sleeping and flopped into the water.

The little telescope showed a small area but it was remarkably clear. Steed surveyed the shrubberies and copses between the causeway and the marsh. Nothing moved except the birds. He examined the two sides of the house that he could see. Many of the windows were obscured by foliage, but apart from a glimpse of Bella Reeves passing a ground-floor casement, those in view provided nothing interesting either. He scanned the turrets and the tower. The former were empty, but there definitely *was* a *camera obscura* in the latter: he could make out the prism and the 360 degree turntable on which it revolved, under a cap on top of the cupola. He couldn't see much to the rear of the building, there were too many trees in the way—but he caught sight once of two men, one short and one tall, crossing an open space between the stables and the house. Later, someone visited the aviaries. He was unable to tell whether it was one of the men he had seen before.

The afternoon wore on. The wildfowl maintained their ceaseless activity. Vehicles passed along the road in each direction. A bank of cirrus clouds appeared high in the western sky, temporarily shrouding the sun.

At five o'clock, the poacher's daughter appeared on her bicycle at the top of the drive. Steed watched her through the spyglass as she cycled to the gates—noticing the leg-lifting routine about which Emma had told him as the machine passed the row of white posts. A few minutes later, he heard the whirring of tyres above and behind him as she pedalled up the road.

At a quarter to six, when it was almost dusk, a light came on in two of the ground floor windows. Shortly afterwards, curtains were drawn across them. The sun, which had dropped into view below the cloudbank for a few minutes before it set, now flamed vermilion accents across the mackerel sky from below the horizon. The constant rising and circling and settling of the birds became more pronounced. As a long skein of Brent geese flew in over the marsh from the sea, Steed decided that the time had come for action. He reassembled his umbrella, adjusted the angle of his bowler and scrambled to his feet.

It was about a hundred and fifty yards from his hiding place to the junction of the dyke and the causeway. Since it would obviously be madness to attempt a crossing of the marsh in the darkness, he decided to edge his way along the foot of the dyke until he reached the wire fence protecting the entrance to the drive. From there, he would cut the corner to gain the higher ground on which it ran, and then work his way up to the house through the shrubberies bordering it. He had about two and a half hours before the moon rose—when he would have to leave to avoid the risk of detection, either directly from the windows or via the *camera obscura*.

The going was relatively easy at first. Stepping gingerly from hummock to hummock, testing every one with his toe before putting his weight on it, he advanced cautiously. Soon, the causeway trees rose blackly against the sky—shading now from the palest of greens along the western horizon to a deep violet in the East. He should run across the fence before long . . . Yes, here it was: an ugly tangle of spiked wire, attached to iron stakes cemented into the marshy ground. It ran from the gateposts to the beginning of the dyke, curved down the bank, and ended about a dozen yards along the flank of the causeway. The only thing was, Steed discovered when he tried to walk around the end of it, that there was a deep pool ideally placed to prevent such a manoeuvre. He decided to examine the wire—and for this the umbrella was once more pressed into service in yet another guise. Beneath the beaker, recessed in the deep rim of the ferrule, was a small electric bulb. Steed took a slim battery from his pocket, clipped it into place below the handle, pressed a button at the top of the shaft—and a pencil beam of light shone from the foot of the umbrella. He poked it in among the strands of the fence and clucked disapprovingly below his breath. Twisted in with the barbed wire at each level were filaments of small-gauge alarm wire—though whether they were of the electrical or mechanical type he was unable to tell. Without knowing this, and with the time neither to track the wires to their source nor to investigate their type, it was obvious that any attempt to disconnect them was out of the question. He would have to retrace his steps, make a cast across the corner of the marsh, and outflank both wire and pool.

Pointing the umbrella at the ground before his feet, he trod carefully back a dozen yards, the thin ray of light illuminating the rough terrain over which he had to travel. It was quite dark now, windless and becoming cool. The faint, high humming of insects had ceased and only the intermittent murmuring and gabbling of wildfowl out on the marsh broke the silence.

Steed shouldered his way through the barrier of reeds and began picking his way across the dark saltings. He jumped lightly over a rivulet, stepped along a shelf of sedge that squelched underfoot, and traversed a firmer area humped with coarse grass. Skirting a bed of rushes beneath which the ground was sure to be waterlogged, he leaped another stream and then turned at right angles to approach the causeway parallel with the dyke. Once his foot slipped as an apparently firm tussock sank beneath his weight; another time, he miscalculated and plunged one leg into eighteen inches of icy water—but his waterproof shoe and sock, bonded together and elasticised to the calf, let none of the moisture in; and the fibres of his seemingly ordinary dark suit were siliconized to make the material as impervious as an oilskin.

At last he approached the silhouette of the causeway once more. He had cleared the pool and the end of the wire well enough. But now there was another barrier: immediately before the firm ground, water had carved a deep channel in the mud—and, even if the marsh had permitted him to take a run at it, this time it was too wide to leap ...

He came to a halt, exasperated, and switched off the eye in the umbrella. He looked to either side: the channel seemed to extend in each direction. Then, on an impulse, he looked up into the air.

About five feet above his head, a branch from one of the big trees on the far side of the water stretched darkly across the sky.

Steed pointed the umbrella at the dim shape and permitted himself the briefest flick at the flashlight button. In the fraction of a second that the beam lanced the night, he saw that the branch, not yet in leaf, looked solid and sound. He reversed the umbrella, gripping it by the ferrule, and then, holding it at arm's length, stretched up on tiptoe and hooked the handle around the branch. After a moment's hesitation, he reached up the other hand, grasped the ferrule firmly and swung himself, Tarzan-like, out over the water . . .

He landed heavily on firm ground, the impetus of his fall pulling the umbrella away from the tree with a scattering of bark and small twigs. A Water Rail, startled from its sleep among the grasses at the edge of the channel, splashed noisily into the water and swam away with a *Quark!* of alarm.

Steed picked himself up and listened. There seemed to be no other reaction to his arrival so, after waiting a moment, he settled his hat more firmly on his head and moved up the bank into the grounds of Turret House proper. The causeway was about eighty yards wide, the drive running straight up the middle. There was therefore a sizeable strip of ground on each side, fairly densely covered with trees, shrubs and an occasional spinney—and it was through these that the undercover man intended to work his way towards the house.

He had no idea whether or not there might be watchdogs— animal or human—staked out around the house or available to come rushing at the call of an alarm. Either "Worthington's men" or the "retainers" could be swarming around him unseen. He must therefore proceed with great caution—and be extremely prudent in his use of the flashlight from now on.

Holding the umbrella, unlit, before him like a geiger counter, he inched forwards into the shrubbery. The ferrule quested this way and that, seeking obstructions that might impede his progress, roots over which he might trip. He had only gone a few yards when it brushed against something a few inches from the ground, not solid enough to be a branch, too resistant for leaves. He probed and prodded experimentally in the dark: it seemed to be some kind of cord or wire . . .

There was a metallic squeak somewhere above his head.

He jumped backwards as a cascade of liquid showered to the ground, splashing noisily on the hard earth and pattering off leaves. Had he not been holding the umbrella at an arm's length in front of him, he would have triggered off the trip-wire with his leg and got soaked!

Risking a flash from the light, he shone the bulb upwards. Yes— a simple schoolboy booby trap: a galvanised bucket pivoting on a rod supported by two branches. When the wire was displaced beyond a certain point, a counterweight tilted the bucket—which spilled its contents on whoever had actuated the wire. It was simple and harmless. But what on earth could

THE HOUSE ON THE MARSH

be the point of dowsing an intruder? Surely no burglar would be discouraged simply by having a bucketful of cold water poured on him?

Water? Steed sniffed. A peculiar choking smell drifted on the night air. He held the umbrella down and pressed the torch button again. Above the drenched ground, leaves were steaming. From a narrow iron band encircling the ferrule, reflected light showed him a curl of heavy brown smoke rising. With a stifled exclamation, he crouched down, sniffed again, and reached out to touch one of the wet leaves. He put his finger to his lips and licked briefly at the moist fingertip. With a grimace, he spat and then rubbed the finger hard on a patch of dry earth.

That was no water. The bucket had been filled with sulphuric-acid!

All right, then, Steed said to himself grimly. At least we know where we are now! The people who had rigged up that particular booby trap were no innocent old gentlemen guarding their privacy...

Plunging the acid-splashed ferrule into the ground to cleanse it, he gripped the umbrella more firmly and went on. He crossed an open space under some trees and came to a thick hedge of hawthorn. Treading with infinite care, he moved along it towards the house until he came to a wicket gate. This time he was taking no chances. Shielding the light with one hand, he pressed the button and examined the gateway minutely. There was no sign of any trip wire. He touched the gate itself. It swung easily on oiled hinges, with no sign of squeaks or creaks. As he pushed it open and went silently through, his toe caught on a root and he instinctively lowered his head and looked down.

There was a vibrant metallic twang and a giant fist slammed him on top of the crown.

Steed was knocked backwards by the force of the blow and sat down heavily on the ground. His ears were ringing and for the moment he didn't realise what had happened. Then, gingerly, he reached upwards and prised the bowler hat off his head. It was a very special hat: both brim and crown were of bullet-proof steel under the furry velour covering. ("But where on earth did you *get* it?" Emma Peel had cried, the first time she saw it. And Steed had replied, smiling: "An idea I picked up from a film I saw—one of those preposterous spy things, you know. But it's a good one for all that...")

Now, sitting in the darkness, he felt the hat all over. There was a dent, two inches across and an inch deep, in the steel crown. He whistled softly and felt around him for his umbrella. Before he found it, his groping fingers touched something else: an eighteen-inch shaft tipped with a murderous iron sphere about the size of a golf-ball.

It was the bolt from a crossbow—and if he hadn't been wearing the hat, or if he had not looked down, it would have gone straight through his head . . .

He crawled through the gate on hands and knees and located the weapon wedged in the fork of a tree. It was operated quite simply: the gate was of the self-closing variety, worked by a weight hanging down inside the hollow gatepost. When the weight rose as the gate was opened, it pulled a wire connected with the mechanism of the bow—and the bow was trained with deadly accuracy on the person using the gate.

Steed's nerves were steelier than most, but the next half hour was a nightmare, even for him.

Turret House was ringed with lethal variants of schoolboy booby traps. A magnesium flare erupted with a violence that seared his eyeballs while he was negotiating a thicket near the drive. Later, he was brought up against another hedge—pierced this time by a conveniently placed stile. He tested the four steps by prodding them with the umbrella. Both of those on the far side collapsed under the slightest pressure, hingeing forward so that the foot of anyone putting his weight on them would plunge downwards to be impaled on a row of wicked-looking steel spikes projecting from the ground below. Steed handled that one by retreating a few yards, taking three quick paces forward, placing the palm of one hand on the rail, and vaulting neatly over the stile.

His eyes had grown quite accustomed to the dark, but it was still extremely difficult to make out details under the trees bordering the drive. From the house, chinks of light still showed between the curtains of the downstairs room he had noticed from the marsh—but there was no other sign of activity, despite what had seemed to him the enormous noise made by the various devices he had actuated. And, of course, the nearer he got, the more careful he had to be with his own small light. He edged his way towards the drive—he was almost there now—between two rhododendrons.

"*All right Worthington: you move round behind. I'll take him here.*"

Steed froze. The penetrating whisper had come from somewhere on the far side of the bushes. He took a firmer grasp on his umbrella.

"*Will do. But don't hit too hard: we want to ask questions.*"

Steed whirled. This time the voice, a different voice, had come from behind. As he waited, tense, a low chuckle came from behind a clump of box hedge clipped into ornamental shapes on his right.

The undercover man took three quick paces backwards and dropped to the ground, lying flat on his face and hardly breathing.

Nothing happened.

The expected rush of feet did not materialise. No blow swished through the air, no flame stabbed the dark.

Steed's fingers had levered a stone loose from the mossy ground. Cautiously, soundlessly, he raised one shoulder so that his arm was free and lobbed the stone towards the rhododendrons. It crashed in amongst the leaves and dropped to the ground.

Silence.

Steed frowned. Slowly, he wormed his way along the ground towards the bushes. He had almost reached them when:

"*All right Worthington: you move round behind. I'll take him here*"—the whisper sounded exactly as before. For the first time that evening, Steed grinned. He did not turn round when the second voice repeated: "*Will do. But don't hit too hard: we want to ask questions*"; he took no notice of the second performance of the eerie chuckle. He got to his feet and walked boldly to the rhododendrons, poking the umbrella in among them and switching on the light.

A tiny loudspeaker was wired to one of the branches.

Obviously the voices were recorded on a tape loop, transmitted via three separate speakers. And the apparatus was set in motion every time anyone passed a certain point—probably by a contact concealed beneath the dead leaves on the ground...

Steed wasted no more time on it and stepped on to the driveway. Just to his right were the twin lines of white posts Emma had told him about. "Apparently there's a yellow line painted in the middle of the drive," she had said, "and Bella's told to get up a bit of speed, lift her feet, and coast while she's between the posts—but she must be very careful to steer exactly along the line. It's some kind of warning device, and they don't want it set off every time she comes or goes..."

Taking care not to pass in front of any posts, Steed examined the place carefully. Yes—there was the yellow line; just like a lane-line on an arterial road. And, as he had surmised, each post bore at the top, on the side facing the driveway, a disc something like a reflector. The discs were faintly luminescent and tilted slightly forwards. This must be a rather elaborate version of the "electronic eye"—a series of photo-electric cells which would actuate some kind of warning system if anything broke the circuit by passing through the invisible rays they emitted. Presumably they were beamed downwards so that there was a narrow "dead area", marked by the yellow line, not covered by the rays from either side. Anything wider than the line—a pedestrian, say, or a car—would be bound to cross one of the rays and set off the alarm. But, provided the feet were kept up off the pedals, the narrow tyres of a bicycle could pass along the line without breaking the circuit. This, however, was essentially a system to give advance warning of "legal" callers coming up the drive; it wasn't one of the anti-prowler series with which Steed had been wrestling! He shrugged and crossed the drive to the far side. Here at least there was a stretch of clear ground under the trees reaching almost to the house. Shouldering the umbrella, he tiptoed rapidly across it towards the lighted windows.

Suddenly he was falling.

The earth had given way beneath his feet and he dropped like a stone into a narrow hole. In a lightning reflex, he whipped the umbrella from his shoulder as he fell, put up his other hand to the sliding collar and opened it.

The erected canopy slammed down over the aperture like a stopper in a jar, bringing Steed up short with a jolt that shook the breath from his body. The special reinforced steel ribs groaned... but held. If they had given way, and his weight had pulled the umbrella inside out, he would have gone on down, taking the umbrella with him. As it was, he hung like a man on a parachute in pitch blackness—his own arm's length plus the length of the umbrella shaft below the surface.

For a moment he gasped to regain his breath. There was the dank smell of moist earth about him. Small pieces of soil and pebbles were still crumbling from the lip of the hole to plop into water somewhere below him. He kicked out with his legs until he found one of the sides of the shaft—then, redoubling his grip on the umbrella, he "walked" himself slowly upwards until his feet were on a level with his waist. From that position it was relatively simple to lower his back until it touched the opposite wall. Then, pressing with feet and shoulders, inch by inch he worked his way up to the top in the manner of a mountaineer negotiating a chimney.

It was only a matter of five or six feet, but the earth was soft and puddingy, giving nothing like the purchase to be obtained from rock. By the time he rolled over the lip of the hole to safety, he was covered in sweat.

He lay still until the hammering of his heart had quietened down, then sat up and reached for the umbrella. First he closed it up, then he unscrewed the handle and drained the remainder of its contents, and finally he tested the button to see if the flashlight was still working. It was. Lowering it into the hole, he saw, about fifteen feet below, the faint gleam of water—through which the points of a dozen stakes whittled to a needle sharpness thrust evilly upwards. At the edge, branches and leaves which had covered it lay scattered.

"A Pooh trap for Heffalumps, by Jove!" he breathed.

He rose to his feet, a scarecrow figure very different from the immaculate Steed who had left the cottage that morning. His shoes were caked with wet mud, his jacket was torn, both suit and shirt were stained with moss and earth and plastered with leaves, and his hat was dented . . .

He looked at the luminous dial of his watch. In twenty minutes time, the moon would be up. He could do nothing more now.

Turning to the dim outline of Turret House, he raised his battered bowler in a theatrical gesture.

"Very well, gentlemen," he apostrophised the unseen occupants. "Your round, I think! . . . But I shall try again tomorrow —though it'll be by a more socially acceptable route, I fancy!"

He clapped the hat back on his head, straightened his muddy tie, and headed back towards the marsh.

11

A GHOST IN A BATTERED BOWLER...

EMMA PEEL was laughing. Under the low roof of the Lotus Elan, she hunched over the steering wheel trying hard to stifle the spasm of uncontrollable mirth which had seized her. From the big, twin dials of speedometer and tachometer subdued dashboard lighting picked out an occasional contour from her black jersey cat-suit and rippled the highlights dancing across the shiny *ciré* insert stretched over her shaking breasts.

"Oh, Steed!" she gasped. "Oh, Steed—one of the slowest entrances you ever made . . . and unquestionably one of the best!"

She had been five minutes early for their rendezvous at the lay-by from which she had watched Turret House that morning. But at the appointed time, there had been no sign of the undercover man. Five minutes had passed . . . ten . . . fifteen. And at last, far down the road, her anxious gaze had caught a movement among the bushes fringeing the dyke near the gates. A moment later, a nightmare figure had burst out on to the road. Like a badly designed ghost, it had been covered from head to foot in shining, dripping white. A white and dented bowler hat crowned its head; white plastered its face, clung to its jacket and coursed down its trousers; and from its albino shoes a trail of white footprints led, clown-like, to the foliage from which it had emerged. Slowly, this apparition squelched down the road towards the lay-by. At last, it drew to a livid halt by the car. In the ghastly mask of its face, matted eyebrows raised and Steed's eyes looked out.

"Enter," he said sepulchrally, "a man in a white suit."

And Emma, dropping her tawny head to the wheel, had collapsed. "Oh, dear . . . I *am* so sorry," she cried. "But really . . . you looked so . . . so *hysterical*—Goodness! My mascara's running!—No, but really, I mean . . ." And she burst into another peal of laughter.

"We are always pleased to be able to entertain," Steed said stiffly. "Perhaps if you could direct me to a convenient television station—commercial, of course—I might be able to turn an honest penny: I must be whiter even than that whiter-than-white fellow."

"Now you're adding brightness to whiteness," Emma said. "But what happened, Steed—what *happened*?"

"I managed to evade a boxful of lethal tricks and fell for a harmless one. Perhaps it's fortunate it wasn't the other way round."

"I don't follow you."

"Your innocent old gentlemen have a bizarre sense of humour, it seems. The place is crawling with booby traps."

"Not the explosive kind, I hope?"

"Not so far as I found out. That doesn't mean there aren't any, though. But concealed pits covered with dead leaves, showers of sulphuric acid, gates which set off crossbows and dummy stiles which impale you on spikes are enough for me. We Steeds can take a hint—and I received a definite impression that I wasn't welcome. Naturally, as a gentleman, I left immediately."

"You didn't penetrate the defences at all, then?"

"No. By the time I was at the house it was too late."

"You still haven't explained about the *white*, though!"

"I do beg your pardon; I had no intention of keeping a lady waiting," Steed said, sweeping off his hat with a theatrical gesture. A quantity of viscous white fluid showered from the brim and splatted on to the Lotus's bonnet.

He surveyed it for a moment. "It's whitewash," he said at last. "It'll wash off—me as well as the car, I hope . . . No—I'd managed to avoid all their tricks, and perhaps I became a little careless on the way back. I went in on the far side of the drive, you know, and came back this side—so it was all new territory, as it were. And just as I got to the bank of the causeway and was thinking that at last I was clear . . . I missed a trip wire and set off this blasted thing!"

"*What* blasted thing, for Heaven's sake?"

"Repeat performance of the Great Sulphuric Acid trick—as carried out before crowned heads throughout the civilised world; and parts, as they say, of Bratby."

"You mean there was another bucket . . . ?"

"Balanced on a plank this time. Full of whitewash. Didn't half fetch me a grievous blow on the shoulder, I can tell you!"

Steed said, rubbing the injured area reflectively. "Anyone for tennis?"

Emma slid across the passenger seat and uncoiled her slim length from the Lotus. "But what are you going to do?" she asked. "I mean I don't wish to seem inhospitable, but—"

"Yes, I see what you mean. Whitewash can be sponged off me, and my clothes can be cleaned—but black leather upholstery's another thing, isn't it? To say nothing of black leather ladies."

"It's black *ciré*."

"Same thing, only less so . . . I tell you what, the only thing is, I'll have to strip."

"To the buff?"

"My *dear!* No—just the outer layer, you know. I'll take off me jacket, trousers, shirt, tie, hat and shoes—and bundle them all in the boot, if you don't mind."

"What will that leave you?" Emma asked curiously.

"Well, socks, of course. And . . ." Steed hesitated.

"Steed!" Emma laughed delightedly. "I do believe you're embarrassed. What is it? Are you wearing a darned vest?"

"No, it's not that, my dear. It's just . . ." The undercover man paused once more. "Well it's just that I thought I might be getting immersed in marshes and things. And so . . ."

"And so?"

"And so, recalling that it was cold for the time of the year, I thought it might be prudent to have something warm underneath. In short, I put on one of those long-legged sort of combination things that one wears under ski clothes. As a matter of fact they do look rather like ordinary combs," Steed said with elaborate nonchalance, "and I'd hate you to think . . ."

"I assure you, Steed," Emma replied gravely, "that *mentally* I shall see that lithe and muscular form clad in the briefest of singlets and jockey shorts . . . What colour are they?"

"Striped, actually. In violet and black."

While he peeled off his whitewash-soaked outer garments, Steed recounted in more detail the trials and tribulations he had suffered in the grounds of Turret House. Finally, before stowing the soggy bundle in the boot, he reached into the inside pocket of the jacket, took out a large gold cigarette case, opened it, and produced two smoked salmon sandwiches wrapped in greaseproof paper. Handing one to Emma and biting a large chunk out of the other himself, he sank gratefully into the Lotus's passenger seat and closed the door. "Now," he said, munching, "let's hear your own report. What have you been able to find out?"

"The undercover man indeed!" Emma said, looking admiringly at the horizontal stripes with which Steed was now ringed. She switched on the car's heater. "You'd better have this on, or you'll catch your death . . . Now, let's see. First, Sir Charles's findings. Doctor Atherley, the porter at the station, the admiral, the political speaker—all of these gave positive tests to the Moraes reaction. They were poisoned, in fact. The tramp you know about . . . Oh, yes—and the Beaknik."

"What about her?"

"Well, according to Sir Charles, that young lady was no better than she ought to be. The poor fellow they found on the Bratby road wasn't the only tramp in the case, it seems!"

"You mean she was pregnant?"

"Had been. An illegal operation was performed shortly— very shortly—before her death. A most *professional* job, Sir Charles said."

Steed whistled. "Maltby, of course!" he said. "No wonder he was scared if he'd just done an abortion and the girl died on him. How *did* she die, by the way? Was it poison again?"

"It was. Teal, this time. A sauce made with the giblets. But so far as Maltby is concerned, there's an additional reason for him to be frightened: according to my researches in the village, there's a three to one chance that he was the father as well. And he's a married man . . ."

"I see. The plot thickens . . . Anything else from Charles?"

"They exhumed one of the earlier seven: an old woman who used to be postmistress at Little Hornham. Positive again. But the insurance man at Boston and my gamekeeper were both negative—unquestionably natural causes, he said. I couldn't shake him on it."

"Don't worry. Statistically there have to be some 'genuine' deaths among them. Otherwise the area would be *below* the national average. And that would be just as odd! Besides, Boston's really outside the area, and Birmingham's on its southerly fringe . . . Did you find out anything at all about our practical jokers?"

"Oh, yes. Your Special Branch friend, MacCorquodale, was a great help there. Warbeck-Simner's apparently quite a big noise in the ornithological world—writes books; contributes to *Field, Ornis, Zoologist, Ibis* and so on; reads papers before the Royal

Society and the French Academy of Natural History. That sort of thing."

"And the Professor?"

"Charnley has a doctorate in pharmaceutical chemistry. He studied at Berne and at Munich before the first war, and he had a chair at one of the red-bricks in the early thirties. But the interesting thing is that he took a degree in toxicology—in South America!"

"Did he, by Jove! Not at your old *alma mater* in Bahia, I suppose?"

"No, he was at Rio, as a matter of fact. But it's interesting— Munich could spell neo-fascist sympathies, couldn't it? And Toxicology in Brazil certainly smells of Curare to me."

"So much for your innocent old gentlemen," Steed said. "If I know old Mac, he'd never let you off the phone without telling you something about their personalities as well. Come on— give!"

Emma smiled. "He stressed that it was deduction and not fact," she said. "It seems that Sir Albert Thing comes from a Very Old Family. Apparently there was some legal tangle, years ago, about descent—and if he'd won he'd be the Earl of Bratby today. Only he didn't and he isn't."

"So he's got the dead needle to the rest of us because we're on the same level as he is—and he feels we ought to be below?"

"That's about it. Plus the fact that he has a thing about the divine right of people like him to govern the country."

"Any fascist, neo-fascist or Nazi connections?"

"No, MacCorquodale didn't think any of them were aristocratic enough."

"And the jolly old Prof?"

"Another embittered man. Originally he went to Brazil because he'd been passed over for some top executive job in favour of a civil servant. *He* thinks the eggheads and the boffins should run the world! Apparently Sir A took a fancy to him and set him up in this plushy lab in the grounds about three years ago."

"H'm. Toxicology, eh? Any fascist connections in his case?"

"Oddly enough, no. None whatever, despite the Munich period."

"And the organisations?"

"Blank. Special Branch have no knowledge of any group, overt or covert, calling themselves The Retainers or anything like it. They have no dossier on anyone called Worthington who might be linked up with our little battle. And they don't even have a file on any likelies."

"Well," Steed said with a sigh, "there's nothing for it but to press my *alter ego* into service."

"Your what?"

"My alias. As a journalist gathering material on migration, it's only reasonable that I should seek the help—and defer to the opinion—of one of the experts on the subject who's actually here. Tomorrow, I seek professional audience of Sir Albert Charles Frobisher Warbeck-Simner. And if he's as susceptible to flattery as your report suggests, it shouldn't be too difficult to get to him . . . But I shall want to borrow this car."

"What's wrong with the Bentley?"

"Nothing is *ever* wrong with the Bentley. It's part of the definition of a Bentley. But there is a special reason why a Lotus will be more suitable for this particular journey."

"What reason?"

"The fact," Steed said enigmatically, "that it is, in the words of a famous Kansas City blues, little and low and built up from the ground. You'll see what I mean tomorrow . . . In the meantime, there's tonight. That wasn't a very big sandwich. Do you fancy driving me back to my pad, waiting while I change, and then taking me to your inn for dinner?"

"I do wish," Emma said crossly, turning the ignition key to start the Lotus, "that you didn't find it necessary to be so infuriatingly *oblique* about things." She swung the wheel over and nosed the car out of the lay-by on to the road. Soon, they were humming along in the direction of Bratby. Just before they reached the gates of Turret House, Steed gave an exclamation of annoyance.

"Blast!" he said. "I've just remembered: I left my umbrella at the bottom of the bank while I was trying to fight my way out of the whitewash. Do you mind pulling up here for a second while I nip down and get it? It's one I'm rather fond of."

"You ended that sentence with a preposition," Emma called after him as he plunged through the bushes and down the bank out of sight.

About three minutes after he had gone, there was a swish of tyres and a large black Wolseley saloon cut in and stopped in front of the parked Lotus with a faint squeal of disc brakes. All four doors opened at once, as a spotlight on the roof swivelled to fix the sports car in its fierce glare. Four large men piled out and advanced on Emma.

Startled—for she had not heard the saloon approaching—the girl shielded her eyes against the blaze of light. For a moment she experienced a thrill of alarm. Then she saw that the men were dressed in police uniforms.

A heavy man wearing a sergeant's stripes on his sleeve came up to the driver's door. "All right, then—what are you doing here?" he began. And then, leaning down and seeing Emma for the first time: "Oh. Excuse me, miss. Routine check, you know ... Do you mind giving me your name and address and showing me your driver's licence, please?"

"My name is Emma Peel. Mrs Emma Peel. And I'm staying at the 'Feathers' at Bratby," Emma replied, handing her licence through the window. "What's up? What are you checking, then?"

"Thank you, Miss ... Madam, that is," the big man said in his soft East Coast burr, studying the little red book. 'We get a lot of poachin' around here, you know. Rascals with no regard for other people's property. You wouldn't believe some of the things people get up to. We just like to keep an eye on things." He handed back the licence. "D'you mind tellin' me what you're doin' here, Madam?"

"I'm—er—as a matter of fact I'm ... waiting for a friend," Emma said, fighting back a desire to laugh hysterically.

There was a rustling in the bushes at the side of the road.

The four policemen swung round. A fifth, in the black saloon, turned the spotlight on to the foliage.

The leaves, silvered in the glare, became agitated. The rustling grew to a crashing. And finally the branches parted as Steed in his glory, dead on cue, appeared—first the chalky mask of his face just above the level of the road, then a hand grasping a piebald umbrella, and finally the splendid length of his combination-clad body, ringed in black and purple, as he climbed the steep bank and burst through on to level ground.

For a moment, he paused—an arresting sight. Then, walking towards the car, "I'm so sorry," he said to Emma. "I didn't realise that we had company."

There was a short silence.

"Would this be your ... friend?" the sergeant asked heavily at last, with a helpless gesture in Steed's direction.

A GHOST IN A BATTERED BOWLER...

"Why, yes," Emma said weakly, dropping her head to the wheel once more, "there he is now!"

The sergeant coughed. "Good evening—Sir," he said, addressing himself to Steed. "I don't wish to appear unduly inquisitive, but might I ask exactly what you think *you're* doing?"

"Good evening, Sergeant. No trouble at all. I just came to fetch my umbrella, that's all."

The four policemen stared at Steed, eyeing him slowly from the top of his head to his stockinged feet. "Came to fetch your umbrella," the big man echoed at length. "Just so. I should have guessed, shouldn't I?"

"No, but really," Steed protested. "I happened to leave it here —on the marsh, that is—at the foot of the dyke, I should say. And then I remembered I'd forgotten it. So I came back for it... Look!"

As though to prove his point, he lifted the umbrella and opened it. A cascade of whitewash splashed to the ground.

The fifth patrolman had climbed out of the police car and was standing with the others looking after them, Emma saw over her shoulder before the road took them into the dip at the far end of the dyke. The sergeant was still slowly shaking his head.

"All right, so I looked funny," Steed said later, as the little car drew up outside his rented cottage. "But I cannot see what you keep on laughing at."

"No, it's not that. It's just—it's just... Oh, did you *see* that poor man's *face*," Emma cried. "And as for you, you don't look funny at all: you look as though you'd just been a ghost!"

12

MATTERS OF MIGRATION

Sir Albert Charles Frobisher Warbeck-Simner placed the palms of his hands on the flat top of his desk. Below the domed forehead, his coarse featured face looked almost benign. "What school did you go to, Steed?" he asked.

Steed told him.

"I thought so," the ornithologist said, looking towards Professor Charnley. "Long after my time, of course. But you can tell, can't you?"

"Oh, yes, you can tell," echoed the scientist. "You can tell alright."

Looking as vacuous as he dared without making a lampoon of it, Steed perched diffidently on the edge of a straight-back chair. He wore horn-rimmed spectacles and his hair was parted at one side. A flat cap was stuffed into one of the huge patch pockets on the skirted tweed jacket he wore. His boots and his Norfolk breeches were linked by a pair of excessively hairy stockings.

"What a treat it is to see a man properly dressed," his host continued. "I can't imagine what a fellow with your advantages is doing messing about with journalism, though: it's hardly a gentleman's profession, is it? ... Still—we mustn't be personal, Charnley, must we! Now ... what can I do for you, young man?"

"Well, sir, I do hope you won't think it a frightful liberty," Steed said, shifting from side to side on his chair, "but I've been commissioned to do this series of pieces—articles, that is—for *Grandstand*—"

"*Grandstand*? That's the picture thing, isn't it? They did quite a decent colour picture of Ospreys at Loch Torridon a month or so ago."

"Yes, sir. That's the one. Well—I have to do this series on bird migrations, you see ... and naturally Suffolk, the Fen District, and round here are the first ports of call, if you see what I mean ... and while I'm here the obvious person to ask—I mean an ornithologist as famous as yourself—if an expert as well-known doesn't mind being quoted, that is..." Steed allowed his voice to tail away shyly.

"My dear boy. Of course I should be delighted. If there's anything I can usefully say, that is. Commander Scott's really *the* authority for this part of the world, you know."

"Yes, sir. Naturally we shall be paying tribute—but if you *would* be so kind, there are one or two things I imagine only you could tell us."

"H'm. Well tell me the general outline of your feature—the direction it's taking; so I'll know the level, so to speak, at which the audience is listening," Warbeck-Simner said, shooting an unexpectedly shrewd glance at Steed.

"Well, basically, the series is informative rather than discursive. That is to say, we presume a near-total ignorance on the part of the reader, and then fill him in on the—er—salient details."

"A fairly safe presumption in England today, I should imagine," Professor Charnley put in tartly.

"In other words," Steed continued, smiling politely, "we tell the reader that this extraordinary phenomenon exists, that the same birds return to the same summer or winter quarters every year, coming thousands of miles across the ocean without food or rest, to the very same pond or shed or hedge. And we give details of how they come and how all these things can be proved by ringing and so on. And how they come every year practically on the same *day*—and how they all get ready for the journey and leave together . . . all that sort of thing, you know."

"But that's the merest generalisation. Any encyclopaedia—"

"Yes, sir. I know, I know—Forgive me for interrupting you! —but that's just the background, as it were. Once they've been filled in we start on some of the more bizarre aspects of the thing. Then we tell them all about the fascinating research—the sort of thing in which you specialise, sir—and round off with as many —er—unusual stories on the subject as we can dig up. It's not exactly a scientific approach, I'm afraid . . ."

"No, it jolly well isn't! Really, I fail to see how I can help."

"If you could just perhaps answer a few questions . . ." Steed began desperately.

"Well, a man doesn't like to be churlish. What questions?"

"Well—let me see . . . I have it here somewhere, I know . . . now where can that piece of paper—Ah! Here it is! . . . Yes.

You have an actual sanctuary here. Do you find this means there is a greater variety of birds than on the normal Fenland saltings? . . . Do you find the fact that it's a sanctuary encourages birds to collect undisturbed before their migration? . . . Does the fact that it's uninterrupted encourage vagrants to stay here? . . . Can you tell me of any special techniques of observation you have developed here? . . . Do you think that winter—"

"Wait, wait, wait—wait a minute, old man!" Warbeck-Simner expostulated good-humouredly. "One at a time, yes? Your first point, now: variety. As a rule there's not too much difference in ordinary migrants. If an oddity *does* turn up, though—we're much more likely to get him."

"I saw something under that heading as I drove along."

"Did you really?" Charnley asked quickly. "What was that?"

"Well, that's what I mean: I couldn't place it. It looked like some kind of duck, but it had a bright red bill and the rest of it was black and white and a sort of auburn colour."

"Where did you see it?"

"Down on the marsh as I came along the dyke. There were two pairs paddling about—then one pair flew off. The wings look very white when they're in the air."

"Jolly good for you, Steed!" the ornithologist beamed delightedly. "Those *were* rather special, as it happens. We just have the two pairs this year—and we're lucky to have them, I suppose. That's *Netta Rufina*: the Red-Crested Pochard, no less."

Steed was scribbling in a small notebook. "Thank you, sir. Any more like that?"

"Well, first of all, you do realise that I specialise entirely in wildfowl, in water birds, do you? You'll hear nothing from me of Stints, or Sandpipers, or Dunlins, or Godwits, or Redshanks, or Buntings, though I am sure most of them are about, if you care to look for them. No—I'll talk to you about these birds, maybe tell you something about them; but I won't *examine* them Steed. I won't *investigate* them."

"What *are* your special interests then, sir?"

"You've been around here some days. You tell me," the old man said, with another penetrating look at the undercover man from beneath his shaggy brows.

"Well I've noticed Mallard and Pintail, of course. And Curlew. And Brent geese and Grey-lags and Pinkfeet. Grebes. Divers. Sheldrakes and Tufted Ducks . . . Let's see—Oh, yes.

and Wigeon and Teal. And I thought I saw a pair of Goosanders one evening."

"You *have* done your homework well, haven't you, Steed? But you saw no Goosanders here: those were Merganser—*Mergus Serrator*, you know. Still, it's a natural enough mistake, I suppose... You were asking about the blessed rarities we get. We have a few you *won't* have seen on the marsh at Bratby—Gadwall, for instance. Shovelers. Garganey and Smew. Even Hodder Ducks and Black Scoters."

"By Jove! One hadn't even heard of the last two!"

"Aha! They're both from the Order *Anseres*, you know—*Oidemia Nigra Nigra* and *Somateria Fuligula* in the Linnaeus classification. But whereas almost all the ducks and geese we get here are winter migrants—flying South from the Arctic to take advantage of our relatively mild winter—these two bracket themselves with the Swallows and Nightingales and other perchers: they're in fact *summer* migrants. They fly up here from North Africa to nest, because it's cooler!"

"But are they here already, then? Is there some kind of overlap?"

For a moment Sir Albert appeared to be disconcerted by the question. He exchanged a glance with Charnley, looked down at his hands on the desk top, and then said rather testily: "Yes, yes, of course there is bound to be a certain amount of overlap at times—not much, mind you, but a little. The earliest of the summer migrants have often arrived and started looking around for nests before the last stragglers have pulled themselves together and flown back to the North, you know."

"Was one correct in thinking you had said the Scoters and—Hodder Ducks, was it?—had in fact already arrived this year?"

"No, no, no. Certainly not." Warbeck-Simner looked quite cross. "I don't know what can have given you that idea at all."

"But one distinctly had the impression that you had *said*—" The vague man with the glasses appeared all of a sudden to have become persistent. The ornithologist cut him short.

"If anything I said gave you that impression, you were mistaken. They're not due for another week or two yet. Now—you were asking earlier about how we observed our visitors..." With the Professor following close behind, he led Steed up one carpeted and three bare and dusty flights of stairs to the observation room at the top of the tower. The second, third and fourth floors of Turret House, so far as Steed could see, stretched away on each side of the landings naked and unused. There was no sign in the dust which lay thick in the corridors of the footsteps either of the egregious Worthington and his men or of any retainers, trusty or otherwise.

The undercover man expressed admiration for the ingenuity of the Victorian forbears of Sir Hugh Mendip who had installed the *camera obscura*. He examined the great ground-glass screen and the little television camera trained forever upon it; he exclaimed at the fidelity of the inverted image swimming serenely in its greens and browns and yellows as the wind stirred the grasses on the marsh far below. He exclaimed in schoolboyish pleasure as Charnley spun the smooth iron wheels and inclined the oiled ratchets to control the prisms at the top of the dark tunnel leading from the observation screen to the open air above. "All the twist controls on the console in the study do," Charnley said, spinning the scanner wheel briskly, "is to duplicate what we're doing now—Look! There's your Pochard! You can pick out the scarlet beak even from here, can't you?—to duplicate what we are doing with rather less—er—effort."

"Even Worthington could hardly do better, could he?" Sir Albert chuckled, taking the scientist by the arm.

The Professor exploded into laughter, glancing slyly at Steed as he moved towards the stairs. "Oh, no," he wheezed. "Even Worthington would be hard put to it—very hard put to it—to better this!"

"Worthington?" Steed allowed a polite interest to tinge his voice.

"Oh, my dear chap!" Warbeck-Simner gasped, dabbing his eyes with a handkerchief. "A private joke. Just a little private jest. You really must forgive me—beastly rude in front of another fellow."

Later, when they had gone back downstairs and looked over part of Charnley's laboratory, the ornithologist succumbed once again to a fit of the giggles and kept nudging the scientist and digging him in the ribs as they conducted Steed over the bird museum.

The old stables and coachhouse had had a lot of money spent on them when Warbeck-Simner first installed his museum there. One wing of the L-shaped block was entirely given over to row upon row of glass cases displaying stuffed birds. Many of the displays were complicated and ingeniously arranged, the suggestions of the exhibits' habitat being especially well carried out.

Ducks, geese and other waterfowl predominated, but there was a considerable section on seabirds, another on land migrants from Africa, and a third devoted to the avifauna of the Mediterranean littoral. In the other wing were Warbeck-Simner's workshop, a fully equipped taxidermy room, a small cartographical section full of cabinets of flat drawers housing distribution maps and migration charts, and what he called the research department. Basically, this was a series of insulated glass compartments in which birds' behaviour could be observed and photographed while such variables as temperature, humidity and atmospheric pressure were manipulated by the experimenter. Beyond it were two more narrow doors, but neither of the two men made any move towards opening them or mentioning what they might hide.

Finally, Steed was shown the aviaries. These varied from small cages in which a tall man would have to stoop to vast, domed edifices thirty or forty feet high. They stretched in a haphazard pattern from the yard, across a neglected garden, and down a slope to the marsh—where a narrow boardwalk led for several hundred yards out across the flats.

"Many of them, as you see, are empty," Warbeck-Simner said. "This is because we do not as a rule reckon to have a permanent collection of foreign birds here—and the native ones you can see, after all, all around you. What we do when we want to —er—examine one of our guests from the sanctuary more closely is to walk out along the catwalk and secure him (or go and fetch him in the Carvel dinghy, for that matter), and then bring him back for a temporary spell in one of the aviaries. As soon as we have finished our researches, the doors are opened—and out he flies again . . ."

A number of the larger cages near the house were, nevertheless, reasonably well inhabited, Steed saw as they strolled back. He noticed Pelicans, Storks, Cranes, a variety of hawks and buzzards, and even a cage shared by a couple of bald, leathery looking birds on long legs and a small flock of Flamingos.

"This migration business now, Sir Albert," he said as they passed a pile of empty bird crates in a corner of the yard. "Tell me: if you went up, say, to the Lake District and netted some birds; if you brought those birds back here and kept them in an aviary; and if—when it was time for them to migrate—you crated them up and *took* them to wherever they come from . . .

when it was time for them to come back here the following year, would they fly here or to the Lake District?"

"To the Lake District, of course. Moreover, if I let them go here before it was time for them to migrate, they go back to the Lake District first. You can't mess them about, you know!"

"And if you kept them here *after* it was time for them to go?"

"As soon as you release them, they go. Right away. We've tried that one, Steed."

"And if you kept them right through the time they're usually away, crating them up and sending them back only a day or two before they would normally have been coming *back* again . . . ?"

"They'd return here on the normal day, just as though nothing had happened—staying the necessary number of days—hours for that matter—in their other home until the time for departure came. But you'll be making your readers' brains reel with these technicalities . . . surely I've said enough? Come, let me fetch you a glass of sherry wine."

Back in the study, Warbeck-Simner produced a very tolerable *manzanilla*. Pouring a small amount into each of three elaborate and rather beautifully chased goblets, he turned to Steed and said conversationally: "You must forgive me attending to this myself; the servant only comes four times a week—and this is not one of her days. Just one more reflection of the sorry state of affairs things have been allowed to come to."

"Oh, you do feel that, too, sir, do you?" Steed picked up his cue adroitly.

"Feel it, Steed? Feel it? One cannot avoid feeling it: it is positively *hammered* into one at every turn, is it not? You and I, Steed—people out of the top drawer—and the brains like Charnley here . . . all the people with *class*, to use an unfashionable word—we're being driven to the wall. And there's not one chap with the beastly guts to do anything about it. Not one, is there, Charnley?"

"Not a single one."

"Oh, I do so concur," Steed said mendaciously. "I simply could not agree with you more. But really, why don't—I mean to say, surely . . . that is to say, couldn't one *do* something about it?"

"Aha! Never give up hope, my dear man. *Nil desperandum* Steed! Beneath the acquiescent surface, things are moving. I'm not at liberty to say more just now—but rest assured, *our* kind is going to come into its own again, mark my words. And when it does..."

"Yes, Sir Albert... when it does...?" Steed prompted.

"When it does," Charnley interposed glibly, "the balance will be redressed at last. By rights, Sir Albert should be the Earl of Bratby, you know. But small-minded people have denied him the rewards he deserves."

"The seventeenth Earl," Warbeck-Simner said, flushing a dull red. "There have been Warbecks and Simners at Bratby and Hornham for over four hundred years. And then, just because some common, cheap, jumped up little jack-in-office of a county court judge decides—" He broke off, choking with rage. "Some people have it in them to rule, to lead; it's bred in them," he added in a strangled voice. "But the majority of our masters today are totally unfitted for *any* kind of responsibility. If I had my way, I'd have half of them put down, destroyed, before I let them anywhere *near* a job where they exercised any control over other men's lives, really I would—I say, look here! My dear chap, your glass is empty! Do let me..."

"Very nice of you, sir," Steed said. "It's a delightful wine. Thank you... but aren't you taking some more yourself?"

"No, no. Charnley and I drink very little alcohol, you know. Bad for the wind—and we've got to keep in tip-top condition, really fit, for this game."

"I'm afraid I don't quite..."

"Out on the marsh, you know," the scientist explained. "We have to keep dashing along the jolly old catwalk to bag the chaps we want to examine."

"Yes—jumping over streams, too. And rowing the old boat about and going for tramps in the early morning. Takes it out of you at our age unless you're fighting fit, dash it all."

A few minutes later, Steed snapped shut his notebook, put it away in his pocket, and bade his hosts farewell with many protestations of gratitude.

"Not at all, not at all," Warbeck-Simner said affably, leading Steed to the front door while Charnley unobtrusively switched on the closed-circuit television set. "Only too glad to help, old chap. Besides, it's so seldom one sees one of *us*, these days... I say, what a funny little motor! What is it? Don't you find it terribly cramped in there?"

"It's a Lotus Elan, actually. I suppose it is rather small—but there's more room than you'd think inside. And it does have its—er—advantages, you know."

"I suppose so. Mind you, we're not frightfully well up in motors. For the few journeys we make into Cambridge or Ely, we find our old Austin"—he pronounced it Orsten—"perfectly satisfactory."

"Yes—well, thanks again. You chaps have been most awfully decent. See you again some time, I hope . . ."

And with a final wave of his hand, Steed ran down the steps of the great portico, strode across to where he had left the Lotus on the far side of the gravelled turning circle, and inserted his 74 inches behind the wheel.

Warbeck-Simner watched the car turn round. Tyres crunched on the gravel, then, with a crisp crackle from its exhaust, the Lotus swung out of sight behind the shrubbery masking the entrance to the drive. He waved again as it reappeared further down the causeway—but the low roof of the car, and his own elevated position standing at the top of the steps, prevented him from seeing if the gesture was returned. He turned and went back indoors to join Charnley at the monitor screen.

"There we are, then," the scientist said as the streamlined shape shot into vision, braked for the entrance, and then nosed slowly out on to the road through the open gates. "He's clear of the premises anyway!" He switched on the second circuit and watched as the *camera obscura* relayed the Lotus streaking along the dyke towards Bratby.

Warbeck-Simner grunted. "I hope the young ass doesn't break his neck," he said. "It seemed to me that the driver's door wasn't properly fastened when he left . . . Anyway, let's stroll down and shut the gates, shall we? We'd better have a look at the retainers, too—we haven't done the rounds today, don't forget."

"Good gracious me, so we haven't! Your young man quite put it from my mind. Yes, my dear fellow—let's go at once . . ."

But the door of the Lotus had been left unfastened deliberately. With the hand-throttle set and the gear lever in second, Steed had rolled neatly out of the car while it was momentarily hidden by the shrubbery, as Emma Peel—after waiting all morning curled up in the space behind the front seats—had slid across to take over the wheel. So far as Charnley and Warbeck-Simner were concerned, they had seen an expected guest step from an apparently empty vehicle; they had seen him get back into it when he left—and they had watched the vehicle itself leave the property. Since cars did not drive themselves, it was obviously a reasonable assumption that the driver had gone with it. And yet —the undercover man reflected—here he was, safely inside the ring of booby-trap defences, undetected and unsuspected. How fortunate that Mrs Peel should have chosen to buy a car whose roof-line was so low that a tall man standing on the steps of Turret House was unable to see who was driving it!

The two men passed within six feet of Steed's hiding place in a clump of laurel and went on towards the gates. A faint smile curved his lips as he watched the tall figure and the short one recede down the long drive. Then, rising silently to his feet, he moved wraith-like through the bushes and sprinted across the gravel towards the open front door.

13

BELOW STAIRS FOR EMMA...
...AND STEED IN A CUPBOARD!

AFTER lunch, Emma Peel drove from her hotel at Bratby to the rented cottage on the shingle spit across the marsh, threading the little car expertly through the winding lanes, past the old Martello tower, and down the rough track behind the storm beach to where Steed's Bentley loomed monolithically against the reeds. She dumped a large paper sack full of provisions on the cottage table, unloaded a quantity of bottles from the Lotus's boot and checked them against a list in Steed's handwriting, and then tacked a big rectangle of thin cardboard over the broken pane in the window.

A thin drizzle was blowing in from the sea as she set off on foot towards the tarred board building where Bella and her father lived. Before she had trudged far through the shifting shingle, moisture was beading her eyebrows, plastering her hair across her face in long strands, and furring with small droplets the black and white concentric circles of a wool beret she had pulled down over one ear. Above black leather boots and trousers, a short white vinyl raincoat glistened as she walked.

Bella and the old man were doing something technical to a length of fine-gauge net draped along the rail of a ramshackle verandah running from back to front of the building. The sea had withdrawn into an oily calm and they must have heard her striding across the stones long before she reached them. But neither of them looked up until she had gained the shelter of the verandah.

Nevertheless, the girl bade her good afternoon civilly enough, and the poacher looked up momentarily to enquire what they could do for her.

"I thought you might like to know," Emma said, "that the results of the other post-mortems we told you about were—in the main—much as we feared they would be."

Reeves grunted. "Don't know why you bothered to come all

this way across the beach just to tell us that," he said. "What d'you expect us to do? Dance for bloody joy?"

"Oh, *Pa!*" Bella Reeves expostulated. "Don't take any notice of him: it's just because he's upset that anything like this could have happened through us, even indirectly."

"No, you miss my point," Emma said. "What I'm really here to say is that we're very much afraid—practically certain, really —that the *moral* responsibility for those deaths may belong to your employers at Turret House..."

"That doesn't surprise me. Forever messing about in that laboratory and then biting a person's head off when you ask a simple question! I *knew* there was something nasty going on there—and if it's ended in people getting killed, the police ought to be called in."

"You're off today: are you going back to Turret House tomorrow, Bella? Is it your day?"

"It's supposed to be. I'm meant to be there tomorrow. After yesterday, though, I'm not at all sure that I'm going to *be* there." The girl stood up and wiped her forehead with a sweatered forearm. Her dark eyes were blazing. "The way those two old monsters treated me, they'll be lucky if I *ever* go back to do their stinking work! Who do they think they are, anyway, treating people like dirt? What gives them the right to talk to you as if you were an idiot, I'd like to know?"

"You're thinking of—er—going on strike, as it were?"

"Yes, I am," the girl cried. "And serve them right, too, if I did!"

"You could help to serve them right quite literally," Emma said smoothly. "If you really wanted to. I mean help to make sure that they got what was coming to them."

"What do you mean?"

"Well, it's all to do with what Mr Steed was talking to your father about the other night, Bella. Mr Steed believes these men are up to no good and he's hoping to catch them red-handed while they're doing wrong."

"I don't see how I can help."

"It's a question of having somebody actually there—of being able to get a person in among them, as it were, to report on what's really going on in that house."

"But *I* couldn't do that. I wouldn't know—"

"No, Bella—listen. You could help by *not* being there—by actually going on strike tomorrow as you intended."

"I can't see how that would help."

"If you stay away and say nothing, just to spite them, all that will happen will be that you'll annoy them. And then you'll be out of a job . . . But if you do it my way, you can kill two birds with one stone."

"What's your way, then?"

"You stay away—but you telephone them and tell them you're awfully sorry, but you are ill. You say you feel very guilty about letting them down—would it be satisfactory if your cousin came on the same days until you were better again?"

"My cousin? But I don't *have* a cousin!"

"Your cousin Emma," said Emma Peel.

* * *

At Turret House, Steed lay low while Warbeck-Simner and Charnley had a cold lunch. Afterwards, from one of the grimy, curtainless windows on the second floor, he watched them cross the yard to the laboratory. Half an hour later, Warbeck-Simner emerged and went into the museum—and in a few minutes Charnley joined him. For some time after that, the undercover man saw nothing of the two men. Then they began to make a series of journeys back and forth between the old stables and a corner of the yard, fetching bird crates and baskets from the stack Steed had noticed on his way back from the catwalk that morning.

They were too far away for him to hear what they were saying —but whatever task was occupying them appeared to be giving them a great deal of pleasure, for they were continually pausing to chuckle and slap one another on the shoulder. While they were thus safely engaged, Steed explored the whole of the second and third floors of Turret House. Not a door on them was locked —and not a single room was furnished, or gave any indication of having been used for decades.

Later, when he had seen the two men head away from the yard towards the aviaries, he ventured downstairs and discovered a small anteroom off the hallway which obviously acted as operations centre for the booby-trap defences surrounding the place at night. There were a number of small tape machines, each with a simple loop in place; there was an actuator fitted with code-labelled inputs marrying up with these; lockers housed measured and tagged lengths of wire in varying thickness, pulleys, guides, bolts for the crossbow, and so on; two huge carboys full of acid squatted in one corner; and there was a centrally placed indicator board equipped with coloured lights. These—duplicated in both the bedrooms upstairs, Steed discovered—corresponded to rooms in the house and various strategic points adjacent to it. The "magic eye" beams must be well placed and cleverly concealed ... for, as he saw with rueful admiration, his own progress from room to room and floor to floor had been duly charted by the different coloured illuminations winking their testimony from the wall. Fortunately there was a master re-set switch, and before he slipped unobtrusively from the house to make his unseen way to the museum, he had erased these electronic witnesses to his visit.

In the old coach house, he found a pile of glass-fronted cabinets awaiting repair and concealed himself behind these to keep watch. The drizzle which had been blowing inland across the marsh in great clouds earlier had now given way to heavy rain, and for the greater part of the afternoon the monotonous drumming of this on the raftered roof far above his head was the only sound Steed heard. There was a small window near his hiding place, and through this he could see a segment of the rear of the property. Charnley and the ornithologist made several appearances on this restricted screen—carrying flat pans of food out to the aviaries, fetching more crates from the far end of the old walled garden, and once—resplendent in oilskins and sou' westers—walking far out along the board path, to return bearing two protesting Mallard, professionally held by the legs. Presumably these had been taken to the laboratory, for when the two men went through the museum later to Warbeck-Simner's workshop, they were again empty-handed.

Steed heard the rise and fall of their voices from the workshop, but he was too far away to make out the subject of the conversation. He was just about to risk a foray to seek a hiding place within earshot, when the workshop door opened and both men came out.

". . . really has got rid of the irritation problem and they don't scratch themselves," Charnley was saying, "then it seems we're past the final hurdle after all."

"Yes. It's just a matter of selecting the species and correlating the dates," Warbeck-Simner said. "The new alloy will be splendid, you can depend on it. But don't tell Worthington!"

Charnley erupted into the usual high-pitched giggle that this name always produced. "On no account," he wheezed. "After all, secrecy and surprise—those are the two elementary factors on which the entire . . ." The remainder of his words were lost as they went through one of the twin doors flanking the workshop and closed it behind them. Before the voices died away into a featureless mumble, Steed had a momentary impression of heat and light and movement as the door opened and closed—then he was once more alone with the rows of stuffed birds looking knowingly out from behind the glass with their beady eyes.

He would have to have a look behind those doors—the doors whose purpose was so ostentatiously not mentioned when he was shown over the museum earlier in the day. But there was already one thing he had found out in the comparatively short time he had been on the watch: Worthingtons and retainers notwithstanding, there wasn't a living soul billeted in the Turret House demesne except for Warbeck-Simner himself and Charnley . . .

* * *

"So, you see, it'll be quite easy, really," Emma said to Bella Reeves. "I'll write down what you have to say on the telephone —then all you have to do is to lend me your bicycle."

"All right, then," the girl said dubiously. "What are you, then, anyway—a detective or something?"

"Not exactly a detective, but something after that sort of thing," Emma replied with a smile. "Kind of semi-official, shall we say?—Which means, by the way, that I shall be handing over intact whatever the old boys owe me for however long I'm there. You can keep the money, just as though you were there yourself."

"But I can't do that. It wouldn't be fair. After all, it's *you* who'll be doing the work!"

"Not at all, Bella. *You* are doing *me* a favour by giving me the chance to get in there. And naturally, I couldn't dream of offering to pay you for a favour—but the least I can do is let you keep the money you'd be earning if you *hadn't* done that favour!"

"I still think you ought to—"

"Besides which," Emma interrupted with a flash of inspiration, "I wouldn't be allowed to keep the money myself, anyway."

"Why ever not?"

"Regulations," Emma said mysteriously.

"Oh. Oh, I see. . . . Well, in that case . . . If you're sure . . ."

BELOW STAIRS FOR EMMA... 103

"Of course I'm sure. I insist. Apart from which, you'll be helping your boyfriend, you know."

"Mark?"

"Yes. Naturally he wants to get to the bottom of all this business of the tainted ducks. He could have been ruined over it, couldn't he?—Well, I mean, look at your own reactions when you thought *we* were after him!"

Bella laughed. It was the first time Emma had ever seen her face animated. Under the full, dark lips, her teeth were even and startlingly white. Her nose wrinkled at each side and a network of fine lines appeared at the corner of her eyes. She was, Emma suddenly realised, quite amazingly beautiful. "It *was* a bit strong, I must admit," she said. "But I didn't realise you were friends of Mark's . . . All right, let's call it a deal. You come down here some time after eight tomorrow morning, and I'll let you have the bike. Now I must be getting along—Mark and I have a date in a half hour."

"I'll run you out there in the car," Emma said. "It's a filthy night for cycling—and you can phone from my hotel on the way."

"Oh, is that the little Lotus? Is that yours?" Bella asked, her eyes shining. "I'd like that very much indeed."

She pulled on a pair of heavy wellingtons and buckled herself into the oilskin blouse she had been wearing when she surprised Emma and Steed disembarking from the dinghy. "If we dash up to the top of the shingle bank and then down the landward side," she said, "we can get a bit of shelter for the walk to your friend's cottage. It's murder along the beach when the wind blows rain in from the East . . ."

Reeves himself having departed on some secret and nocturnal mission some time before, she locked the plank door before turning her storm collar up round her ears, smiling at Emma, and stepping out into the weather. Together the two girls, the white and the black—Emma lean and elegant as a greyhound, Bella as voluptuous as a ripe apricot—bent their heads against the stinging rain and ran across the shining stones. Behind them, through the dusk, wind now tumbled the sea in jagged lines of ivory as the waves broke along the shore.

* * *

It was nearly seven o'clock before Steed could satisfy himself that his unwitting hosts were safely at dinner. In the notebook he had used during his interview with Sir Alfred that morning, he had also copied from the indicator board the disposition of all the "magic eye" beams guarding the approaches to the house. With this to guide him, he was able to work out a route by which he could flit between the laboratory, the museum and house, without revealing his presence, while Charnley and the ornithologist were engaged elsewhere.

The two old men should be at least an hour over dinner, he estimated. This should give him time to investigate those doors near the workshop at the far end of the museum. He jumped down from the window ledge from which he had seen the meal begin, slipped across the wet cobbles of the yard, and re-entered the museum, brushing the damp from his tweedy suit. Two large stacks of crates, each labelled with the name of some bird, now ranked themselves against the wall outside the doors—and the doors themselves were open. Both of them, to his surprise, led to a common lobby—and from this a flight of stairs led downwards to the most astonishing of all Turret House's surprises. On each side of a small office/anteroom, enormous display windows gave on to two zoological "natural habitat" rooms —and both of them were seething with hundreds and hundreds of live wildfowl.

The rooms were vast—far bigger than Steed would have imagined possible, even with the excavations which must have taken place. There was a strange and dreamlike quality about them, an other-worldliness and an almost science-fiction *ambience* which divorced them from the drab realities of the wet evening above as effectively as the armour-plated glass partitioned off their controlled atmospheres from the raw chill of the old stables. Heat and light blazed behind the glass of the left-hand room; between sand and rock, deep-channelled water fringed with exotic flora teemed with bird life—there appeared to be dozens and dozens of them. Several colonies of goose-like creatures stood about at the edge of the water, wagging their stumpy tails from side to side and nattering; two varieties of duck—one with a distinctive blue-black head and a bright crimson bill—waddled up and down the shelving sand or floated somnolently upon the surface; and seeded in among these were a number of tall and elegant wading birds, beautiful black and white shapes with long, upturned and curved beaks. On the outside of the glass, in the fashion adopted by aquaria and museums, small cards identified the species within—although there was of course no means of marrying a particular card with any one of the many birds in sight.

There were four cards. One, headed *Order: Anseres*, read: GARGANEY ("Sarcelle d'éte"). *Anas Querquedula*—and carried underneath the legend *Lea Valley/Clapton/Hoddesdon/Fairhaven . . . 3-6/IV*. There were two cards headed *Genus: Oidemia*. One was labelled BLACK SCOTER ("Macreuse"). *Oidemia Nigra Nigra*; and the other HODDER DUCK ("Canard Quiroule"). *Somateria Fuligula*. Both of these captions carried a superior classification again reading: *Order—Anseres*. A fourth was labelled *Order—Limicolae*, with underneath the words: AVOCET. *Recurvirostra Avosetta*. The distribution legend beneath said *Halvergate Island/Birmingham . . . 29/III*. Both Hodder and Scoter ducks was identified as from *Ely/Waltham/Boston/Fairhaven/Tummel*. And the date in each case was given as 31/III—5/IV.

Grey was the colour predominating in the right hand room. The vegetation and décor was that of the tundra—mudbanks, sedge, reeds and thin channels of cold-looking water. Steed was able to recognise all four species of ducks massed along the water's edge: Gadwall, Teal, Pintail and Common Pochard. The labels outside the glass added the information that the Teal complemented the Garganey inasmuch as it was known in France as "Sarcelle d'hiver"; that the Pochard was of the genus *Nyroca*; and that all four species were to be found in localities described as *Lea Valley/Clapton/Waltham/Tummel/Bristol/Walberswick/Ely*.

Steed whistled softly as he read the legends, copied the names, dates and other data into his book, and studied the panels outside each room which controlled the temperature, pressure, humidity and air movement inside. He was just about to climb the stairs and make his way back to the house when the door of the museum opened. Footsteps crossed the floor, another door was opened—and feet began to descend the stairway to the two "conditioning" rooms. Steed glanced around him desperately. Although he had no misgivings about handling the two old men, both together if necessary, it was absolutely vital that he should not be discovered at this stage of the game. His eye fell at last on a tall, steel stationery cupboard beside a desk placed to command both rooms. It was unlocked—and beneath the lowest shelf there was a sizeable space. In a flash, he was in, crouching down, and pulling the door shut from the inside.

Whoever it was coming down the stairs reached the bottom, hesitated by the observation windows, and then crossed the room to the desk. There was a shuffling of papers, the squeaky scratch of a pen. In a few minutes, more footsteps descended the stairs and a low-voiced conversation began.

Only a few sentences had been spoken before Steed realised for the first time that Sir Albert Warbeck-Simner—and probably Professor Charnley, too, for that matter—was hopelessly insane.

After about ten minutes of talk, both men went back upstairs and out into the wet darkness "to take a dekko at the traps," as Sir Albert said. As soon as he heard the outer door close, Steed slid out from the stationery cupboard and made his way back to the ground floor. There was—he was almost sure he remembered—a telephone on the bench in Warbeck-Simner's workshop. If only it should prove to be an outside line . . .

He was in luck: the number in the centre of the dial was different to that in the study; the workshop did have a separate line. Smiling slightly, he pulled the instrument towards him, lifted the receiver, and asked the operator in a low voice for a London number.

* * *

Bella arrived in Mark Lurchman's private suite at the "Ely Cathedral" as black and as glistening and as frisky as a seal. The hotelier was standing looking out of the big double windows at the rain when she burst in. He swung his short, broad-shouldered body round and held out his arms as she hurled herself across the room at him. "Oh, Mark!" she exclaimed. "Oh, darling, it's good to see you! How are you? What have you been doing? Is everything all right? Has there been any more trouble about—"

"Just a minute, just a minute, just a minute!" Lurchman laughed, holding her off at arms' length. "One thing at a time, Bella. Hold hard and give us a chance to kiss you Hello, then!" Placing his strong, square hands one either side of the cold, slippery stiffness of the oilskin, he drew her slowly towards him again and kissed her warmly on the mouth.

"Oh, never mind about my silly questions, Mark," the girl said, leaning back and staring at his face. "Just let me look at you and hear you say everything's going to be all right." She seized his hands, held them together with her own, and laid her flushed and rain-wet cheek against the dark hairs outlining the backs of his fingers.

"Of course everything's going to be all right," he said gently. "I can't see what you're worried about . . . Oh, Bella darling! Really you are the most beautiful—quite the most beautiful creature . . ."

He brushed the drenched hair back from her forehead with one hand and then cupped her face in his palms as he gazed long and intensely into her smouldering eyes.

"You're earlier than I expected. Who was it gave you a lift in that sports car?" he said possessively at last.

"That was Mrs Peel—you remember, darling: the girl who came to dinner here with that man Steed on that awful evening—"

"Of course. I saw Steed yesterday, as a matter of fact. There's —er—something he'd like us to do for him."

"Us?"

"Well, yes. You and me—more strictly, perhaps, the society."

"The film society? What on earth has the Boston and Hornham Amateur Film Society to do with Steed? Why doesn't he leave us alone? I've already helped Mrs Peel . . . probably more than I should. Mark—I don't want us to get mixed up in this, whatever it is."

"Bella, we haven't much choice. Or at least I haven't."

"Why not?"

"Well—Steed did me a favour once, years ago. A very big favour, as a matter of fact. And he's been good to me about this wretched affair of the duck. You don't think we wouldn't have had a lot more trouble from the police if he hadn't pulled strings, do you?"

"I suppose not. But—"

"Darling, I have to help him. *You* don't have to if you don't want to—the decision's entirely yours."

"If you're in it, Mark, so am I. It's us as a *thing* that I don't want involved—not me personally . . . Anyway, what do we have to do?"

"Very little, actually. It will be good practice for us—and it *should* have the extra advantage of ridding the neighbourhood of something very nasty indeed . . . if Steed's right. And if it does come off."

"Yes, but what *is* it, Mark? What will be good practice?"

Lurchman laughed his deep laugh, his blue eyes twinkling

brightly behind the great blade of his nose. "We simply have to set a little scene," he said. "Very good exercise in ingenuity. We have to create an atmosphere, to arrange a set—and make it one hundred per cent convincing..."

"What scene? What atmosphere?" Bella asked, interested in spite of herself.

"Steed's got to let me know. But it'll almost certainly involve the use of all the arc lights we have, the limes—and we may even have to take The Brute."

"The *Brute*! What on earth's that?"

"It's the in-group name for that enormous bloody spotlight thing we bought second-hand from the film studios last month."

"Oh, *that*... Well, what do we have to do with all these?"

"Transport them across some ridiculously difficult terrain and set them up secretly on location—and then play out a little scene as extras. It's not going to be at all easy."

"It begins to sound fun, Mark. Tell me more—and who's going to be in on it? Not the whole society, surely?"

"Good God, no! That's what's going to make it difficult. Just you and me—and your father... Steed's apparently got round him some way or another!... and a bloke Steed's bringing up from London to help work the lights when we've got them all in place. Plus Steed himself and Mrs Peel, of course."

"What do we have to do as extras? And who are the principals?"

"Depends on the scene Steed wants set. Just loll about in the middle distance and lend local colour, as far as I know. So far as the principals are concerned, these are going to be your—er—employers, though they won't know it, and me!"

"You?"

"Yes. Apparently I shall have to find some excuse to persuade the old boys to take a drink with me—several drinks in fact! Pure type-casting, of course: I shall simply be playing myself!"

"But Mark, it sounds fascinating! What about Steed, though? Where does he fit in? Do tell me more."

"I fancy he prefers to hover about in the background—in effect he'll be directing, as it were. I can't tell you any more, because I honestly don't know what in hell it's all about."

"Well, what shall *I* have to do, then?"

"So far as I know, I think you have to sit about looking glamorous in a bikini—a part you're *well* qualified to play, my pet. Talking of which, for God's sake get out of those things!

Our dinner'll be almost ready—and what's the point of your keeping sprauncy clothes here if you're not going to wear 'em?"

Bella grinned. She unbuckled the glistening oilskin and hung it up behind the door. "Help me off with these boots, Mark," she said, "and then I can dress in a fitting way for your food. May I use your bedroom?"

"Be my guest."

He crossed the comfortably furnished room to a heavy sideboard, poured himself a whisky from a cut-glass Waterford decanter, pulled a cord to draw the floor-length curtains across the windows, and stood sipping reflectively as he listened to the rain hammering at the panes.

"Hook me up, darling?" Bella Reeves was back in the room, unconcernedly manhandling one full breast into the cup of a black satin brassière. She held the edges of the garment together behind her back against the pull of the elastic, backing up to Lurchman so that he could manipulate the fastener. From the waist downwards, a crimson tie-silk dress lasciviously hugged her heavy thighs, its scanty top falling forwards while she fixed the bra. Lurchman set down his glass and took the two elasticated edges from her fingers, his pulses quickening as he pulled the material against the swell of her moist, cool flesh. Minutely, his eyes followed a cascade of tiny black hairs tracing the course of her spine. And suddenly he released the brassière, his hands snaking round to the front of her body to cup the breasts as they quivered free. The nipples were hard against his palms as he spun her round to face him and sunk his mouth on hers. Her tongue flickered between parted lips and her hands came up behind his shoulders to cradle the back of his head as she swung herself against him.

"Oh, Mark," she breathed. "Oh, Mark—don't do this to me ... the dinner—we'll be late for your dinner!"

"Don't worry," he panted, kissing her on her upturned eyes, "in honour of the coming Spring, both the first two courses are cold ..."

* * *

By eleven o'clock, most of the ageing members of The Club— that gloomy establishment hiding behind the Nash portico near Prunier's in St. James's Street—had tottered down the curving staircase and sent the porter in search of a cab. One reading lamp still cast a pool of light into a corner of the funereal smoking room, however. Into it, from two of the shabby leather armchairs with which the room was dotted, there projected two pairs of legs—each pair stretched out, crossed at the ankle, and clothed in dark blue trousering bearing a faint chalk stripe. The rounded toecaps of two pairs of black shoes winked brightly under the electric bulb.

"Extraordinary thing," the august voice of the man called His Nibs said from the shadows behind one pair of legs. "Most extraordinary—in fact I'd never have believed it if I hadn't heard it from young Steed meself. Extraordinary!"

There was a deep sigh from somewhere on the far side of the pool of light. And in a thick Highland accent, on the exhalation of the breath, the single syllable:

"Aye."

"I mean to say, it's all very well, Mackinlay," His Nibs continued in an aggrieved tone, "but if these two old fools were to get away with their crackbrained scheme, there'd be the very devil to pay. The very devil."

"Aye."

"Young Steed's just told me—had him on the telephone not more than an hour ago—he's told me the whole story. Mind you, I knew something very fishy was up as soon as we heard the first reports on all these so-called heart attacks. But I never realised it'd be quite as bad as this."

"No. Ye'd hardly be realisin' that."

"D'you know what these two rascals are planning, Mackinlay?"

General Mackinlay was Head of Security, from which exalted but elastic position he had the twin tasks of keeping the country sane and on even keel—and carrying out the wishes of His Nibs.

"Ye did mention it over tea," he said drily now. "But likely ye'll be givin' it a wee bit goin' over again."

"That rogue Charnley has synthesised this vicious derivative of Curare and evolved a soluble, crystalline form that can be moulded into pellets..."

"Aye."

"... And they're going to stow pellets in the ankle rings on these damn birds when the birds are due to fly here from wherever it is, and the blasted creatures'll fly over and land in our reservoirs and paddle about—and the poison'll dissolve, and ... and Bob's your uncle!"

One pair of ankles in the lamplight uncrossed themselves,

then recrossed the other way over. "How can they tell the birds'll fly to our reservoirs?" General Mackinlay asked. "From over there, I mean."

"Because they've nabbed the birds over here while they're *on* the blasted reservoirs, that's why, Mackinlay. They visit a reservoir they want to poison, just before the migrants are due to leave for, say, Morocco—or Stavanger, for that matter. And they bag these birds and *keep* 'em here all the time they would normally be in Morocco or Stavanger or wherever—keeping them in artificially simulated conditions matching whichever of those places they come from. Then, just before the birds are due to fly *back* here, they ship 'em out home and let 'em loose. Sure enough, promptly on schedule, the birds'll fly over—and there you are."

"Why not go out there and prime the birds with poison just before they left, instead of keeping them here all winter?"

"Because, you great loon, they couldn't identify which of the millions of birds there were coming *here*! It's only by getting them from the target area, as it were, that they can be sure of hitting it again. They go to and from the same places every year, you know."

"Aye, I know. Forbye—"

"The only other thing they could do would be to put the poison in place just before they *left* here—but it would never last all the while they were away: it'd merely poison all the people in Norway or Morocco. And the aim of the operation, Steed says, is to poison all the people in London. And Birmingham. And Glasgow and Edinburgh and Chester."

"Aye."

"I must say, that fellow Warbeck-Simner was pretty damned odd at school. He was years junior to me, of course—but one heard things, you know. They filtered up . . . Still, I never thought it'd come to this!"

"Likely ye'll be wantin' a platoon of men to go in and clean the place up then?"

"Well, no—not yet."

"But for why?"

"Various reasons. Steed says—and I agree with him—that it's no earthly use just nabbing them both. That would stop them going off with one set of birds—but would it necessarily end the operation? We don't know. There may be confederates, here or abroad. There may be other birds, more poison, somewhere else..."

"Aye. I suppose so."

"Steed wants to trick them into giving away the whole crackpot plan—catch 'em red-handed, as it were—so that we *know*, absolutely, that we've got the whole shebang in the bag. Apparently the balloon's due to go up any time now—and his own scheme's mad enough to work, in theory at least. It's the only kind that would, I fancy—because both these chaps are batty; absolutely barmy, the pair of them. Must be."

"Aye. But ye've no told me just *why* we've all to die from the poisonin' like this. What's to be gained? Whose cause are they advancin'?"

The second pair of feet moved: they jerked abruptly back out of the circle of lamplight as His Nibs sat forward in his chair and rested his forearms on his knees. A gnarled hand with a pipe in it appeared in the radiance. "That's just it, Mackinlay," he said vehemently, stabbing the stem towards the lean, lined face he could barely see in the shadows. "We simply do not know. We have no idea, and that's the truth of it. This is why I've agreed to allow Steed to go ahead with his plan to expose the whole dratted thing."

"Aye. Maybe... But would it no be better—"

"The only leads we have to possible accomplices or organisations have both resulted in dead ends. There's nothing else we can do. Perhaps I'll be asking you later for your platoon—even if it's only to stand by. For the moment, I'm sending Benson up to help Steed, and that's it."

General Mackinlay sighed again. "Aye," he said. "But I still have a mind—"

"Oh, Mackers, for Heaven's sake dry up!" His Nibs said crossly. "The trouble with you, my dear chap, is that you talk too much... Now come on: leave it to me and have one for the road. *Parsons!*—Two more large whiskies, please..."

* * *

At five minutes to nine the following morning Jim Reeves loaded a quantity of dead birds into the panniers of an ancient motor cycle; Benson swore moodily as he waited to thread a Land Rover through a blocked roundabout on the North Circular Road; Bella Reeves turned warmly over in bed and bit Mark

Lurchman on the shoulder—and Emma Peel arrived outside Turret House on a bicycle.

She dismounted by the massive brick posts flanking the drive and wheeled her machine towards the centre portion of the wrought-iron gates. There was a small button inset in the metal. A second after she had pressed this, a sharp click presaged a crackling of static before a disembodied voice rasped: "What is it? What do you want, please?"

Emma leaned forward and spoke into the louvred steel box attached to the inner side of the gate. "It's Emma Peel, sir. Miss Peel who's cousin to Bella Reeves—I'm deputising for her while she's ill and it's her day today. I think she's telephoned you about me. May I come in now?"

"Ah, Miss Peel! Yes, of course, Bella did telephone about you. Most kind of you to help us out. Most kind... You're—ah —very punctual, my dear; very. Yes—come up at once, come up. Did Bella tell you about the yellow line?... She did?... Splendid! In you come then..."

An instant later there was a buzz from the mechanism controlling the lock, and Emma pushed open the gate and wheeled the bicycle inside.

Two hundred yards down the road, screened by the bushes masking a lay-by and out of range of the *camera obscura*, Steed yawned, stretched, and rose from the back seat of the Bentley where he had been sleeping since he had emerged from the bird sanctuary just after midnight. He sat on the wide running board and reached for his binocular case. From the velvet-lined interior, he removed, instead of a pair of field-glasses, two cylindrical packages wrapped in brown paper...

Opening the first of these, he took out a miniature thermos flask filled with hot coffee. When he had undone the second, two hard boiled eggs in greaseproof paper, a buttered *brioche* and a twist of blue paper containing salt were revealed. Finally, he fished in his pocket and produced a small leather case about the size of a packet of cigarettes. He placed this beside him on the running board and turned a milled wheel projecting through the hide. "... o'clock News," a voice said softly within the case. *"There has been another rail disaster in Arizona. At Chequers last night, the Prime Minister received members of the cabinet, following..."*

Smiling contentedly, Steed began to peel an egg.

14

EXIT A JOURNALIST!

AFTER finishing his breakfast, Steed plugged an electric razor into a socket on the Bentley's dashboard and shaved. The wind had freshened during the night and blown away the rain clouds. Now beneath the high, pale sky the cold breath from the East scoured the shingle and spilled over the dyke to undulate the reeds and grasses of the marsh in long ripples. From the lay-by, over the thrashing tops of the bushes which formed his own protective screen, he could see branches tossing in the grove of trees around Turret House.

He unlocked the long mahogany box below the Bentley's nearside running board. This had originally been designed to house a superior tool chest, but like certain other parts of the old car had been somewhat modified by its present owner! From the lengthy cavity within, he drew out a fitted dressing case which had been specially made to measure, snapped open the clasps, and took from it a carefully folded charcoal suit, socks, tie, underwear, shoes, and a self-striped silk shirt in cream. It was not yet ten o'clock and traffic on the road was light. Behind the angular bulk of the Vanden Plas body with its erected touring hood, he was easily able to change in the lay-by. When he was completely dressed, he packed away the clothes he had been wearing before, took a high-crowned bowler hat and an umbrella from the back of the car, and re-locked the wooden box below the running board. Finally, he took down the hood, zipped the tonneau-cover over the Bentley's open body, padlocked the zipper tag to a ring on the scuttle, and walked, whistling, towards the gates of Turret House two hundred yards down the road.

At first there was no answer when he pressed the metal button in the gate. He paced up and down, clasping his umbrella behind his back and listening to the roaring of the wind in the treetops, while he wondered whether to have another go. He was just approaching the gate for the second time when he heard the familiar crackle, followed by Emma Peel's voice:

"Yes? Who is it please? Whom did you want?"

Steed leaned down towards the louvres. "My name is Steed. I am a journalist. Sir Albert kindly granted me an interview yesterday. I was wondering—as I had discovered a couple of supplementary questions—whether he would have the great courtesy to grant me another five minutes of his time?"

"Just a moment, please, Mr Steed. I'll enquire." There was the sound of distant voices mumbling, and then:

"Hallo? Steed? This is Charnley here. I'm afraid Sir Albert is not available for a few minutes, but I'm sure he'd be only too —er—delighted to see you. Why don't you come along in and wait?"

"Thank you very much, Professor: that's frightfully decent of you. It'll take me several minutes to get up to the house anyway, as I'm on foot."

"What did you say?"

"That I'm on foot."

"God bless my soul. On foot. Well, well, well."

There was a buzz from the lock and Steed pushed open the heavy iron gate and walked on to the causeway. Considering the amount of lethal machines concealed in its narrow width, it was amazing how innocent the strip of shrubbery and trees on each side of the driveway looked, he reflected as he tramped, swinging his umbrella, up towards the house.

Charnley had said nothing about yellow lines, so presuming he was supposed to be innocent of any knowledge of alarm systems, he walked deliberately to one side of the road when he came up to the double line of white posts linked by chain.

He had no sooner passed the first post than complete bedlam broke out all around him. The noise of Bloodhounds baying ullulated deafeningly from the shrubbery on all sides; frenetic yappings and the deep, growling barks of a Doberman sounded from nearer the house; there was a determined crashing in the undergrowth behind him; and over all, from all quarters of the compass, came the sound of a confused and unintelligible shouting. It was really most effective. Had he not known that the whole performance was simply a series of pre-recorded tapes set off by a "magic eye" beam and relayed through different speakers dotted about the grounds, Steed felt, he might well have been tempted to flee!

Charnley was waiting for him at the top of the steps. "My

dear young chap," he exclaimed, shaking hands, "you really must forgive me. I completely forgot to switch off the dogs of war. Must have given you a devil of a shock."

"The dogs of war?"

"Cry havoc, you know, and let loose the same. Just a little private joke—but come in, come in. I do hope you weren't scared."

"Not at all. Just a little surprised—especially as I could see no dogs, bellicose or otherwise."

"Ha, ha. Bellicose is good. Very good. I must tell Sir Albert. He'll be down in a moment, by the way. In the meantime, is there anything I can perhaps help you with?"

Steed had decided to pay this second visit in his rôle as journalist simply to see if he could possibly surprise some hint from one of the inmates of Turret House about their intentions. Birds of the summer migration were due to start arriving at any time now—and if they intended to crate any of those he had seen in the rooms below the museum, and take them either to North Africa or the North in time to release them for the flight back to England, they would have to be packing up and leaving in the immediate future. But it was vital to Steed to know when they were to leave, which place they were going to, and what species they had decided to use. Only with this information—in the event that he failed to spring the whole plan first—could he deduce the probable dates of arrival of birds carrying the poisoned pellets; for each species arrived each year on precisely the same date. And only with this information could he work out, from the notes he had taken in the conditioning rooms, which reservoirs the chosen birds would be likely to land on when they did come. He had therefore nothing to lose—and perhaps something to gain—by "stirring things up." So he replied to Charnley's query by saying:

"Not in connection with migration, thank you: there are just a couple of simple questions I have to ask Sir Albert. But you might be able to help me—or rather a friend of mine—on another matter."

"Really?" the Professor said warily. "What is that?"

"I believe you are a toxicologist of some note, sir, and that you studied in Brazil?"

"That is so. But I fail to see—"

"This friend of mine is a doctor, sir. He has diagnosed no

less than seven recent deaths in this neighbourhood as being due to a poison deriving from South America."

Charnley had gone quite pale. "Really, Mr Steed, I cannot for the life of me think why you should imagine I could be of any help," he stammered.

"If you studied toxicology in Rio, Professor," Steed continued remorselessly, his vague and diffident manner suddenly evaporating, "I imagine you must be familiar with Curare?"

"Indeed. Yes, of course I am familiar with it. An Indian drug."

"What would you say were its main characteristics?"

"Well . . . I—I . . . Well, I suppose that it totally paralyses all muscular activity, especially of the diaphragm and thorax—"

"Thus inhibiting the circulation and the action of the lungs so that the victim dies very quickly of asphyxia?"

"Er—precisely. Without losing consciousness, as it happens. The French have often used it as an extra anaesthetic in surgery. Its advantage is that it can aid surgery by making the patient *totally* relax the muscles—of the stomach, for example—and thus facilitate incision and manipulation."

"And its disadvantages?"

"That it is difficult to calculate accurately the very small amounts required—and that it is possible, without realising it, to operate on a *conscious* patient, since he cannot move a muscle to tell you of the agonies he is suffering . . . But what on earth has this to do with your friend and his diagnoses?"

"Does the word Helimanthine mean anything to you, Professor?"

Charnley had gone a ghastly colour. Beads of perspiration stood out on his upper lip and his forehead. "What—what— how dare you cross-examine me, sir!" he blustered "What, pray, do you know of Curare and—and Helimanthine?"

"I'll tell you," Steed said affably. "I know that Curare was discovered by Europeans soon after the discovery of South America in the late fifteenth century. I know something very like it was mentioned by Homer in the *Odyssey*. I know that it is an extract of the juices of a diversity of plants, the exact blend of which is a carefully guarded secret. And I know that Humbold saw it being prepared in 1800. Do you know about Humbold, Professor?"

"He said it was a mixture of vegetable juices and saps, cooked together and evaporated, filtered through a cone of banana leaves and then concentrated again," the scientist said sullenly. "And he also reported that the natives found the resulting concentrate too—er—runny, I suppose you'd say—for their purposes, so that they had to mix it with some bituminous substance to make it stick to the heads of their killing arrows and darts."

"Exactly. And because all the Curare we got in Europe was this sticky, bituminous concentrate, it was awfully difficult for the medical johnnies to separate out the active ingredients or measure accurate doses for clinical purposes. Until Bohm isolated Curarine—the active constituent of Curare—in 1912; and then proceeded to synthesise it chemically, so the profession no longer needed to rely on the import of supplies from Brazilian witch-doctors who wouldn't let them into the secret of its manufacture."

"So you can read an encyclopaedia, Mr Steed. I fail to see what this has to do with me, or why you should presume to come here—"

"I mentioned Helimanthine, Professor. How would you define that?"

"It's a—a—a synthesised drug. It's in effect a highly intensified version of Curarine ... a hundred times more deadly and with the added advantage that it's soluble in water. But it's enormously difficult to make because several of the ingredients themselves never occur in a natural state and have to be synthesised first. Why—why are you so interested in this rare substance, Mr Steed?"

"Because the seven deaths my friend diagnosed were all due to the ingestion of Helimanthine, Professor ..."

"Very well, Charnley: tell Mr Steed all about it!"—The voice boomed out from the doorway, where Warbeck-Simner's tall figure stood outlined against the light—"Tell him the truth: that you and you alone succeeded in synthesising Helimanthine where all the others failed; that we have succeeded, again, in manufacturing it in crystalline form; and that, via our friends the birds, we intend to use it to relieve this beautiful island of ours of many of the vermin at present infesting it ..."

Steed swung round in his chair. "That's a very challenging statement, Sir Albert," he said. "It could almost be taken, by those with mass homicide on their minds, as a veiled threat."

"I'm a challenging man, Steed, as I should have thought you

might have realised by now. But I uttered no threat: merely a statement of fact."

"I'm afraid I don't quite understand."

"I think you understand very well. Nevertheless, I am prepared to dot the i's and cross the t's if you wish. First, though, let us take some coffee." He crossed the study to a hanging bell cord and pulled it. In a suspiciously short length of time, Emma —wearing a white vinyl apron over a simple black jersey dress, with no make-up and her auburn hair caught back in an Alice band—was standing in the doorway.

"Ah, Peel. We'll have the coffee now, if you please," Sir Albert said. "There will be one extra, as you see."

Emma bobbed down in a curiously old-fashioned parody of a curtsey and turned to leave, as Steed became the sudden victim of an apparent attack of coughing. The tray must have been waiting immediately outside the study door, for she reappeared instantly and began to hand round the cups and saucers.

"Thank you, Peel," Steed said gravely. "That smells very good."

"Thank *you*, sir."

"Very well, Peel: that will be all. You may go," Warbeck-Simner called, stirring his coffee as he moved across to his desk. "Now, Steed—you wish me to commit myself, no doubt?"

"I didn't say so. I was merely dashed curious about that remark of yours concerning the vermin, you know. If I were a news man instead of a feature writer—"

"*If* you were a journalist at all, Mr Steed. I think we can drop the pretence, if you don't mind. It will save you the embarrassment of trotting out your beastly little vacuities in an attempt to convince me that you are less intelligent than is the case; and it will spare Charnley and myself the tedium of watching you make a fool of yourself."

Steed made no reply. He sat, relaxed and well back in the chair to which Charnley had shown him, with his eyes fixed on the ornithologist's face. His umbrella stood between his knees and his hands were crossed over its handle. The bowler hat lay on the floor beside his chair.

"Were you a journalist," Warbeck-Simner continued evenly, "you would indeed have a story fit for a news department. For I tell you categorically that I intend to destroy the population of the greater part of London—and that of many other cities and areas as well."

"Why?"

"As a lesson. The fools have permitted the reins to fall into the wrong hands. Those whose mission it is to rule, to govern, to direct the lesser ones into paths where their meagre talents may most usefully be employed—they have been pushed aside. And the time has come to redress the balance. But first there must be a drastic purging, a cleansing, before I move in to assume responsibility."

"You're mad. Quite mad. You do realise that?"

"Madness is relative, Steed," the big man said coolly. "What was insane yesterday is normal practice today; what is madness to you and the great majority of unimportant people is perfectly sane to me. Besides, that is a quibble, a matter of semantics—what matters is the *fact* that I shall do as I planned."

"I see. It would, as you say, be a very good story. What makes you imagine that—even if I am not a journalist myself—I won't use it?"

"The fact that you will not be leaving here alive."

"Oh. Might one ask why?"

Warbeck-Simner picked up a photograph from the desk. "You're a fool, Steed, as I said. I confess I'm most disappointed in you. I had thought from your conversation at our first meeting that we might have much in common—but now I see that I was deceived, wilfully deceived. You have been poking and prying and peering into things which do not concern you—and like all nosey parkers, you must pay the penalty. Regrettably, Charnley and I had been dilatory in going the rounds of our little—ah—protective devices on the occasion of your first visit. Otherwise we would have known that some intruder had been blundering about on my property, and the evidence of your duplicity would have been to hand."

"Evidence?"

The ornithologist turned over the photograph in his hand so that Steed could see what it portrayed. The background was totally dark and the foreground was blurred with a moving branch—but between the two, arrested in a pose of astonishment, a man in a dark suit and bowler hat faced the lens with an umbrella held like a sword. Unmistakably, it was Steed himself.

The subject of the picture now smiled faintly. "Not a very good likeness, I'm afraid," he said. "The flash was in my eyes... I suppose the camera was automatically exposed when the trip wire set off that magnesium flare?"

"Certainly it was." It was Charnley speaking now "There's not a device in the grounds that doesn't have a purpose. You don't suppose the flare's put there just to startle you, do you?"

"I suppose not. Silly of me not to realise that. I should have guessed from the quality of the other—er—devices."

"The whole episode was silly—a reckless and immoral escapade which is going to cost you your life," Warbeck-Simner said severely. "I will not tolerate trespassers violating my property. I will not tolerate interference with my plans. And most of all I will not tolerate deceit."

"Assuming that one has been found guilty on those charges, is a condemned man allowed a last wish?"

"Condemnation, charges, guilty—these are terms implying a court, a trial, fixed penalties for a particular verdict arrived at by a given set of rules. There's no question of that in my system. I just decide if a given person is to be punished—and if so, how."

"'I'll be judge, I'll be jury, said cunning old Fury; I'll try the whole cause and condemn you to death'," Steed quoted softly.

"Precisely. You make my earlier point for me: much of Lewis Carroll's so-called nonsense is in fact profoundly sensible if looked at from the right point of view."

"The point of view of a monomaniac or a madman, for instance?"

"Relative terms again, Steed. You will not succeed in needling me. I have, after all, every card . . ."

"Then surely you'll not miss one. Deal it to me and grant that last wish—it's only for a piece of information. And you did promise to dot the i's and cross the t's, you know."

"What is it, then?"

"Tell me which species you are going to—er—honour with the task of being the harbingers of your brave new world. Which birds'll be the carriers of death?"

"I haven't made up my mind."

"Ask me another! Very well, then—who is Worthington?"

Charnley gave a little crow of laughter. He exchanged glances with Warbeck-Simner—and for a moment the big man, too, allowed a brief smile to soften his arrogant features.

"Worthington, Mr Steed?" he said. "Why *you* are Worthington. It's a private code-name we invented for Them—for all the meddlesome, shortsighted and narrowminded fools who try to thwart the beneficial designs of superior intelligences such as Charnley here and myself. But, as you see, the day of reckoning for the Worthingtons is at hand. So far as you yourself are concerned, we have a pair of nesting eagles in a rather special aviary. They are vicious and ruthless in defence of their young—and they have been kept, I regret to say, hungry. What a pity such an engaging fellow should stray into their cage during a trespassing expedition!"

"I'm not too hot on the straying, actually," Steed drawled lazily. "You'll have to get me there, you know."

"Fortunately that contingency has been—er—provided for," Warbeck-Simner replied. "You presumed a moment ago to bandy a quotation with me. Here is one for you. *Thou wretched, rash, intruding fool*—farewell!"

As he spoke the last word, he pressed a button set in a platen on his desk.

For Steed, the room and the two old men in it abruptly whirled down to his feet and spun away into darkness as the armchair in which he was sitting tipped silently backwards on a hidden trapdoor and precipitated him down a slanting chute.

There was a brief rush of darkness, sensations of bruising at elbow, head and knee, and then he was brought up on level ground with a jolt that knocked the breath from his body. As he scrambled automatically to his feet in bright light, he heard from somewhere above the soft thud of the trapdoor swinging back home.

"*Hamlet*, Act III, Scene IV, by Jove," he murmured as he looked about him. He was on the floor of an underground aviary—an earthed area about twelve feet by twelve which formed the bottom of a shaft more than twenty feet deep. There were steel bars lining the sides of the shaft, and these continued up beyond its lip, forming a dome of about the same depth which projected into the open air. At one side of this, there was obviously a caged passage communicating with another aviary—for through an opening as Steed gazed upwards a giant bird hurtled with a scaly flapping of wings. It was indeed an eagle—and at that moment, seeing him, it plunged downwards into the shaft with a scream of rage...

The umbrella that the undercover man found himself still grasping was his only weapon—and although it was steel shafted and steel handled, in other respects it was perfectly normal.

He backed against the steel bars of the cage, his eyes fixed on the descending bird, his mind, ice cold, drained of everything but the vital necessity of keeping at a distance from it. A single blow from one of its wings could break a limb, a twist of that cruel beak would lay flesh open to the bone, a convulsion of its claws could rip through sinew and tissue as easily as a butcher's cleaver through a hanging carcass.

Against the solid, barred wall of the shaft, he was a difficult target. For a moment, the eagle hovered, flapping, and then it struck downwards with claws outstretched. Steed was waiting. Delaying it until the last moment, he thrust violently and rapidly upwards with the ferrule of the umbrella, between the bird's rigid legs. The steel shaft struck the softest part of its belly, just below the breastbone—and while it was too blunt to penetrate the covering of strong feathers, the force of the blow, plus the enormous momentum of the eagle's striking descent, made an impact sufficient to send Steed sprawling to the ground and the bird reeling to the far side of the shaft, squawking its dismay. The secret agent was on his feet like a cat. In one fluid flow of movement he had hurled himself across the floor of the cage and leaped on the eagle before it could flounder into the air again. There was a brief maelstrom of movement, a flurry of arms, wings, feathers and legs—and then the steel handle of the umbrella had been crooked around the bird's neck, the shaft twisted once sharply in a certain way . . . and the great bird was no more a menace than the examples of the taxidermist's art which enlivened the corridors of the museum above.

Steed turned from the inert bundle of feathers to meet the attack of the eagle's mate, which was now winging with cries of fury from the opening leading into the aviary above. He could not use the same defence a second time, for the collision had buckled the long tip of the umbrella and it was no longer sufficiently inflexible to have the same effect. As the bird dropped down the shaft, he crouched in the angle of wall and floor, erecting the umbrella and holding it shield-wise above his head and shoulders.

The outstretched talons struck the taut nylon like a thunderbolt.

The whole of the umbrella's canopy vanished instantly in a criss-cross of black tatters. Steed was holding onto the shaft like grim death, however, and the charge did not succeed in wresting it from his hands.

The eagle wheeled in a tight circle and came in again. Again the shock of the impact almost knocked Steed to the ground. But, as before, the construction of the umbrella prevented the bird from getting to close quarters. When it struck for the third time, Steed adopted a different tactic. Rising slightly on his toes, he jammed the umbrella upwards as the wicked talons hurtled down towards its battered frame. Then, just as the iron-hard claws penetrated the remaining shreds of fabric, he twirled the shaft to entangle the curved toes and heels in the complications of the umbrella's ribs.

The ruse worked. The eagle's feet were fast caught in the damaged framework of the umbrella. With a great beating of wings, it sought to gain height. It was immensely strong—so powerful that its efforts nearly lifted the undercover man from the ground and the two of them, the man and the bird linked by the ruined umbrella, bounded from side to side of the shaft in a kind of grotesque slow-motion ballet. Finally, Steed could hold on no longer: he released the shaft and dropped his aching arms.

Freed of his weight, the bird bobbed upwards, flapping its wings thunderously as it fought to free its talons from the mesh of steel spokes.

Steed gasped for breath and reeled against the wall—then suddenly saw, to his astonishment, a length of hawser which had certainly not been there before dangling down the opposite wall of the shaft. It came into view over the lip of the hole into which the aviary was sunk, and reached almost to the floor. And it was still spiralling slowly from side to side, so it must only just have been dropped.

With a wary eye on the floundering eagle, he edged round the side of the cage until he reached the rope. Then, bracing his legs against the wall, he shinned up hand over hand. The bird was still blundering about all over the aviary, but it was obviously more interested in freeing its feet than in attacking him.

As he drew himself up to the lip of the shaft, he came face to face with the anxious countenance of Emma.

"Thank goodness!" she exclaimed as she opened a small wire door in the side of the cage and helped Steed through. "I was afraid we'd never get you out!"

Steed was dusting off the knees, elbows and shoulders of his suit. "I'm much obliged," he said formally. "Just where are those two murderous old rogues now?"

"Quite happy to leave you to a fate worse than whatever. They informed me that you had left and then went over to the laboratory."

Steed looked around him. The domed aviary from which he

had just emerged was one of a group of several isolated cages off to one side of Turret House. He had not particularly noticed it when he had been shown round the property the day before. Not far off, the old walled garden sloped down to the marsh.

"Does the laboratory have any windows facing the back of the property?" he asked.

"No, it doesn't."

"Good. Then I can make my way to the board-walk that leads out across the marsh without being seen."

"Yes—but hurry, Steed. They may be booby-trap-minded, but they do have duck guns, you know! If you run out right to the end of the catwalk, you'll find an old dinghy there. Don't try to get back to the dyke road; forget about the Bentley. You can collect it later. Head straight away from the house—there's quite a deep channel and the marsh isn't nearly so extensive that way. The old boys use it whenever they fetch supplies: it brings you to a landing stage just off the Ely Road."

"Splendid. Next time they can swim for it, then!"

"And Steed—what about *this*?" Emma said, gesturing towards the aviary and the giant bird still flapping inside it.

"Oh—leave the doors open and let him go. He's earned his freedom. Then our hosts can either think I'm Superman, or that he was a super eagle who's taken me off to his mountain eyrie. You can alibi yourself all right for my—er—miraculous escape, can you?"

"Yes, yes. I'll telephone you if anything at all seems likely to break . . . I assume the plan we arranged still goes through?"

"Of course, my dear. And I've a little chore to keep you amused while you wait for our friends to make up their minds."

"Really? What's that?"

"There was a rather splendid limerick which began with the challenging lines: *A vice both bizarre and unsavoury / Was that of the Bishop of Avery* . . . I've forgotten the middle bit, but it ended up with something concerning an underground aviary. In view of recent experience, I was wondering whether you might not bend your talents towards the composition of a version that was a little more—shall we say?—topical," Steed said lightly. He waved his hand gaily and ran down the path between the cages towards the marsh.

15

OPERATION WORTHINGTON

FOR four days after Steed's escape from the eagle, nothing happened. Deliberately, in case she might be under surveillance, he kept away from Emma during the time she was not working at Turret House. Across the marsh, life in Bratby followed its sleepy routine. Benson arrived in the Land Rover and put up at the "Ely Cathedral" with Mark Lurchman. And Steed himself lay very low, not knowing what channels of information Warbeck-Simner and Charnley might have in the village. Most of the time he spent on top of the storm beach with his field glasses—a position from which he could command most of the surrounding area visually and yet still hear the telephone in the cottage if it rang. He saw Reeves and Bella several times down at the far end of the spit, busy recaulking and painting a boat, attending to their nets, and performing mysterious services for a variety of birds and beasts running about outside their shack. Benson and Lurchman bumped down the track in the Land Rover one afternoon to discuss certain arrangements with him. And a fierce gale blew up from the North in the night, dragging great breakers up from the shallow sea and pounding the shingle beach so that the darkness was filled with the thunder of waves and the rattle of receding stones.

The telephone rang just after lunch the following day. The wind had died down but the sky was overcast and lines of white capped rollers still marched in obliquely to the shore from the North. Steed was actually in the cottage and had scooped up the receiver before it had had time to shrill twice. Emma's voice sounded strained and anxious.

"Steed? It's on. They leave tomorrow morning."

"Ah! Peel, isn't it? I trust you're liking it in service."

"Look, Steed, don't—we don't have time for pleasantries. I've been given my notice and paid off. I'm supposed to be leaving right away and I can't find any excuses to stay here—I may have to put down the phone at any time if one of them comes back into the house. Alright?"

OPERATION WORTHINGTON

"Right, my dear." His voice was all at once alert and crisp. "Tell me what you can. Where are they going, first?"

"Morocco. They've put it about that they're going on holiday to Tunisia, but I managed to get a look at the air tickets. They're travelling by one of the charter lines—and they've booked two dozen crates of livestock as freight on the same plane."

"Have they indeed! If it's Morocco, then those crates will contain one or all of the species in the hot-room under the museum . . . No sign which one, I suppose?"

"No, none. But it'll hardly be all. The hot-room birds are all crated up—and there are *seven* dozen crates! I think they still haven't made up their minds which to take . . . But the birds from the cold-room have already been let loose—I can't *tell* you what a confloption that made!"

"One can imagine! . . . All right. We'll put Operation Worthington into action—starting, as the Americans say, as of now. You leave as soon as you like and cycle to your pub. I'll pick you up there later on . . . You did manage to execute all those little— er—commissions about the house that I dreamed up, did you?"

"Yes, I did."

"Excellent. Do you know what time tomorrow—"

"Steed!" Emma's voice was low, urgent and hurried. "There's someone coming. I must go now . . ." the receiver was quietly replaced.

The undercover man hung up and hurried out to the Bentley. There was a great deal to do—and not much time in which to do it. His plan to find out which species were to be used was daring and crazy. But it might work—so long as the wind held off and it didn't rain . . .

Half a dozen miles away across the flat countryside, two hands —one small and feminine, the other, on top of it, large and masculine—pressed down on the telephone receiver in the study of Turret House.

"I was too late to hear whom you were telephoning, Miss Peel," Sir Albert Warbeck-Simner said menacingly, "but I think you and I had better have a little talk . . ."

* * *

At dusk that evening, a strange convoy set out from "The Ely Cathedral." In the lead, Steed's vintage Bentley carried beneath the cover zipped over the rear seats an inflatable rubber dinghy, a couple of duck guns, two suitcases full of certain "props", and a half dozen cardboard boxes containing seven-inch spools of tape. In the passenger seat beside the undercover man Jim Reeves sat with his hands nervously clasped around his knees. Behind them, still wrapped in overcoat and muffler, Benson piloted the Land Rover with Bella Reeves beside him. The back of the vehicle was loaded to the axles with studio flood- and spot-lights on telescopic stands with cast-iron bases, a jointed framework for a semi-cyclorama, a huge roll of nylon for the screen itself, a 35 mm. film projector and three cans of stock, and a quantity of semi-tropical plants in pots. Bringing up the rear, Mark Lurchman's E-type Jaguar—which carried only a case of Champagne apart from its owner—seemed almost dull by comparison.

The three vehicles headed South until they reached the left turn for Bratby at Little Hornham church, when Steed pulled in to the side of the road and waved the others down. He got out of the Bentley and walked back to the Land Rover.

"This is where we part company for the time being, Benson," he said, leaning in at the window. "Mr Lurchman and I turn off for Bratby and the road along the East side of the marsh here. You carry straight on until you hit the Ely road—and that skirts the West of the marsh."

Benson sighed heavily. "I suppose you do know what you're doing, Mr Steed," he said. "His Nibs said to give you every help. But if you ask me ... all right, all right; I know you *don't* ask me! ... if you did ask me, I'd say it was the most harebrained scheme—even for you—that I'd ever heard of! It's crackers! It's bloody mad ..."

"Madness is best met with madness," Steed said. "You've viewed your unloading place, haven't you? It's pretty well sheltered there, so you shouldn't be bothered—but if anyone does ask, you're a second unit from a film company, on location, right?"

"I suppose so, Mr S."

"Right. Now you know what to do when you get there. We'll rendezvous with you at exactly eight fiftyfive. Mr Lurchman goes in at nine prompt. And we start the ball rolling by signal at twenty past."

"I can't for the life of me see what you can gain by it, sir," Benson said morosely. "Mark my words, no good'll come of it; it'll never work. Not in a hundred years."

"Come, Benson—let not your honest countenance be sicklied

o'er with the pale cast of thought. Yours not to reason why and all that jazz."

"That's as may be, Mr Steed. But I owe it to His Nibs to—Oh, well ... never mind. It's all water under the bridge, I suppose ..."

"That's my boy! If there *is* any doubt—geographically, I mean—Miss Reeves'll put you right ... All set, Bella? You're quite happy about your doubling role, are you?"

"All right, I suppose. But not to say *happy*," Bella Reeves said, leaning across from the passenger seat to look up at Steed. She was a striking sight—white teeth flashing in a face made swarthy with three careful applications of She-Tan. "What I'm worried about is Mrs Peel. You still haven't heard anything?"

"Not a word. We shall call in at her hotel as we go through Bratby—just in case. But I'm very much afraid our hosts for tonight must have become in some way suspicious. In which case she's no doubt still lodged at Turret house..."

"Oh, but how awful!"

"It's a risk one takes," Steed said seriously. "She knows very well how to take care of herself. All the same, I'd be much happier if I knew she was out of there ... if, indeed, she's ever going to get out of there now," he added half to himself in a low voice.

"It seems somehow ... wrong—to be setting out like this, I mean—when we've no idea what's happened to her," Bella said.

"Believe me, Miss Reeves, our little expedition is much more likely to help her than sitting back and just waiting—but don't worry before you need to: I shall probably find her sitting in the 'Feathers' scolding me for being late!"

There was no sign of Emma Peel at the inn in Bratby, however; nor had they any message from her. Reluctantly, feeling very much more despondent than he cared to show, Steed clambered back into the Bentley and pointed its aristocratic radiator in the direction of Turret House.

He pulled up under a clump of trees just before the road ran out on to the dyke. Lurchman's E-type coasted to a halt behind.

"We're taking off from here, Mark," Steed said. "Reeves says it's the best place, despite the distance from the causeway. I suggest you push off and wait in that lay-by I told you about. It's—let's see—yes: it's eight twenty now. Give us an hour. If you arrive at nine as expected, that'll give you twenty minutes to set the stage ..."

As the twin tail-lights of the Jaguar dwindled away down the straight road, Steed and the poacher stripped and changed into lightweight, black rubber frogmen's suits. They darkened their faces and pulled on black gloves. Then, having inflated the dinghy, they piled into it the boxes of tape, the guns, the suitcases and their clothes, before taking one side each and carrying it off through the trees.

"I'm sure you know this marsh like the back of your hand," Steed said as they negotiated a stretch of Alder bushes on the far side of the trees, "but is it really the quickest way of getting to the house, starting right out here?"

"Bless you, yes," the old man replied. "You go in near the causeway, where you did the other day, and you get swamp, you get reeds, you get waterlogged sedge, you get your grassroots all undermined and boggy. Takes you hours to get anywhere . . . But you go in this end, you'll see, you can *use* the boat! There's a fair channel, you see—for them as knows where to find it— which takes you right out to the middle of the marsh from here. You can get to within a hundred yards of the house. Mind, the last bit's tricky, but you're practically home by the time you reach it, aren't you?"

They were walking down a slope now, stumbling on the rough ground and hoisting the laden dinghy over low scrub with some difficulty. The night was windless and cool, the stars hidden by a high overcast. The waning moon was not due to rise for several hours. Steed found it almost impossible to see, but the poacher appeared to be familiar with every bush and each clump of grass.

"Mind, now! Let her down a second," he said after they had gone another fifty yards. "Shouldn't be far from here."

They lowered the rubber boat to the ground and Reeves dropped to a crouching position to line up some private landmark with what meagre lightening was afforded by the night sky. After a moment he grunted. "Thought so. We should be another ten yards or so to the left . . ."

Picking up the boat again, they moved across slowly. Then again he halted, listening. Quite clearly, Steed heard the sighing of the waves on the shore, away on the far side of the dyke. "Right. We'll let her down, then, if you're ready," Reeves was whispering. For a moment the undercover man couldn't see what he meant—then gradually he realised that, immediately before their feet, the ground fell away to a grassy lip. And that under the lip, sombre and mysterious, was water.

The dinghy rocked giddily as they stepped down into it through a screen of bare branches, but as soon as they had pushed it out from under the overhanging trees, it lay very steadily on the channel. Steed sat in the stern while Reeves, who had unclipped a paddle from the bulbous gunwale, crouched at the other end sensing his way across the marsh.

It was an eerie experience. Steed felt no sense of motion at all. The poacher dipped the paddle and directed the craft with uncanny delicacy. Patches of deeper blackness loomed up, passed and dropped astern as they threaded their way through banks of reeds and islands of floating vegetation. At one point the channel widened into a small lake and Reeves waited for several minutes, apparently listening. It was very still. But from every side, Steed gradually became aware, there rose a low sussurrus of noise, a constant ebbing and flowing of staccato gutturals just above the threshold of audibility. It was the gabbling of the innumerable wildfowl across the sanctuary as they settled for the night.

Eventually, the poacher stiffened, craning towards the bow of the dinghy. "Got 'em!" he whispered. "I was listenin' for the Pinkfeet. We have to keep to the left of the mudflat they're on. Hear 'em rabbiting away out there?"

Steed obediently listened—but he could hear nothing ahead of them which distinguished the nasal muttering of hundreds of birds from that behind or to either side. How Reeves could not only identify a particular species but use the noise it made as a direction beacon to "home" on was beyond his comprehension.

The old man sank his paddle noiselessly into the water again —and sure enough a long, low bank of mud soon drew alongside the starboard quarter of the dinghy. Steed could dimly make out the bulk of the big geese, shifting and twitching, as they glided past. A few minutes later, a whisper of sound in the air resolved itself into the rush of wings just above their heads. Hundreds of birds, flying very low and very fast, streamed over uttering a strange *whee-oooo* call as they went—a wild, unbirdlike noise which exploded out of the night like the shrill whistle of a rifle bullet. Steed's hands itched for the duck guns stacked in the bow.

"Wigeon," the poacher commented laconically. "Flighting inland to their feedin' grounds. They're late tonight. Must have been a long way out . . ."

Above the dark mass of a reed bed to their right, the head-lamps of a car lanced the sky over towards the Ely road. Somewhere a long way away, a dog was barking fretfully. And then—startlingly close—there sounded the piercing and mournful cry of a Curlew.

"Ah, that'll be Bella," Reeves exclaimed with satisfaction. "It's the signal. Means they've landed the first load successfully. I'll just confirm that we're doing all right, too." He cupped his hands and raised them to his mouth.

For the second time, the haunting call floated out over the desolate marsh.

* * *

"Oh, good—that'll be Pa. They must be between the Pinkfeet and the Pintail," Bella Reeves panted. "Do you think this old tub'll take the rest of the stuff in one more load?"

"I'm sure I couldn't say, miss. As you know, I regard the whole bleeding enterprise with . . . misgivin'. That's what: misgivin'." Benson scratched his head and looked at the broad-beamed rowing boat tied up at the outer end of the board walk leading to Turret House. "We'll have a shot at it, anyway," he said dubiously. "Anything rather than have to make a third journey!"

They had had no trouble so far. The boat had still been at the landing stage where Steed had left it after his escape from the aviary. Benson had managed to get the Land Rover to within a few feet of the rotting wooden jetty. And they had contrived to load aboard all the lights but one for the first trip, filling in the gaps with the potted plants and the cans of film. Bella had poled the boat across the channel and successfully found the end of the catwalk in the dark. And they had laboriously manhandled the equipment along the narrow board pathway to dry land. It was parked now at the lowest limit of the old walled garden which sloped down to the marsh at the back of Turret House—and all that remained before they started Phase Two of their task was to bring across the remaining spotlight, the projector, and the cyclorama and its framework. Benson, however, having stepped off the board walk in the dark while he was carrying a heavy lamp base and soaked his trouser leg to the knee, was disposed to find difficulties where none existed.

In the event, the rest of the stuff fitted quite easily into the boat and they managed the crossing without incident. It took them a long time to manoeuvre the projector along the narrow walk—

but at last it was done, and they relaxed, breathing hard, with all their cargo safely landed.

Phase Two consisted simply in carting the equipment up past the aviaries and the laboratory, through the yard, and to a flagged terrace which ran along the south side of the house. This was more a matter of time and care than anything else, for Bella knew which route to take to avoid the trip-wires and "magic eyes", and the whole route was along brick paths which were relatively flat. "All right, then," she said at last. "It's twelve minutes to nine. We'd better get started . . ."

*   *   *

The lights of Turret House were showing through the screen of trees which surrounded the property when Steed and Reeves got to what the poacher called "the difficult part" of the journey. Here, the channel they had been following twisted away to the West to join the one leading up to the end of the board walk further out in the marsh. To get to the dry ground of the causeway, they had now to cross an open swamp—a boggy area completely waterlogged, but with the liquid only just covering the saturated ground, too shallow to float even the flat-bottomed rubber dinghy.

"Walking's the only way, I'm afraid," the old man said with a sigh. "And it's as mucky as all get-out—that's why I insisted we had these frogman things. Follow me over the side . . . but don't be alarmed when you sink in: the bog only goes down to about mid-thigh depth at the most. It's good and hard beneath that. And the best part of it's only about eighteen inches . . ."

The swamp was only about fifty yards across. But, as Steed soon found out, the poacher was right in considering it the worst part of the whole journey. As soon as he had climbed over the side of the boat and put his weight on his foot, it sank slowly into the quagmire, to fetch up against solid ground when the surface was at his knee. To take a step, it was necessary to haul leg and foot out of the sucking bog, raise it up above the surface, and then plunge it squelching in again a pace away. The consistency was far too thick for wading—and progress was thus analogous to stepping over an interminable series of hip-high hurdles . . . with the suction of the swamp as an added obstacle to rapid movement. In addition, since the surface moisture was too shallow for towing the dinghy, even without their weight in it, they had perforce to drag it bodily across the tangle of submerged grasses and waterlogged sedge. By the time they reached the far side, their muscles were shuddering with fatigue and they were slopping with sweat inside the rubber suits.

Between the swamp and the high ground on which the house was built lay a pool. They pushed the dinghy across, wading through the water to clean off some of the heavy mud which clung to their legs from ankle to hip. The pressure of the cold water creeping up the skin-tight latex struck clammily against their heated pores and they were glad to start work on dry land again to stave off the effects of the chill night air on the flimsy suits.

Methodically and in silence, they hauled the boat out of the water, stowed its paddle, and vanished into the trees with the guns, the suitcases and the boxes of tape.

They had landed very near to the house: only a dozen yards separated them from the gravelled sweep before the front door. Steed now took charge. He had been content to leave everything to Reeves while they were crossing the marsh: the man was a genius in his field—but now that he was back in his own métier, he automatically assumed command. "Keep right clear of that shrubbery—and avoid all bushes like the plague," he whispered. "You'll be okay if you keep to that clear patch down the centre. But watch the gravel. And don't pass between the portico and the edge of that outbuilding: there's a 'magic eye' beam connected to an alarm guarding it . . ."

Between them they achieved a lot in a very short time. Under Steed's direction they disconnected a number of booby traps and trip wires, dismantled several loudspeakers and re-hung them in different positions nearer to the house, Reeves paying out wire from a field telephone spool to connect them up with the old installations—and finally approached the building itself, where Steed made various strategic alterations to some of the alarm wiring. Mainly, this consisted of running tap wires to an earth peg which he pushed into the ground at the foot of the wall. As soon as it was finished, he turned to Reeves.

"They should be all set on the other side of the house," he said. "Would you like to check, just to make sure?"

The poacher nodded. He cupped his hands again and dropped his mouth to the thumbs. This time, it was the mewing cry of a Little Owl which split the air. And almost immediately it was returned—a sharp sliver of sound piercing the night from somewhere over the roof.

"Splendid!" Steed breathed. "As they seem to be there without incident, I gather Mrs Peel must have been able to attend to certain things I asked her to, before she was surprised by our hosts. In which case it should be safe for us to tiptoe round and join them..."

Noiselessly as shadows, the two men slipped around the corner of the house and across the yard behind, their shining black suits and dark faces virtually invisible against the sombre bulk of the building. On the far side of the house from the study, the flagged terrace was reached by a flight of shallow steps. It ran the width of the place, bordered by a stone balustrade, and below it was a lawn formally sectioned by gravel paths. It was here on the terrace, and in the space between the balustrade and the trees at the far side of the lawn, that Operation Worthington was to be staged...

Bella Reeves and Benson were waiting for them at one end of the terrace, the equipment neatly stacked along one wall.

Steed drew the party together and briefed them. "Everything's fine so far," he said crisply. "But we've a hell of a lot to do now in a very short time indeed. Let me take your tasks in order. Bella—you go to the museum and get the birds. Flamingo, Ibis, Egret, Hoopoe, Mediterranean Shearwater, Phalarope, and that little display of Crossbills and Desert Bullfinch... Right?—Mrs Peel should have left the various cases unlocked for you. When you've brought them, arrange them and the plants in the way we discussed. Then wait here for me and I'll let you indoors to change...

"Benson—you arrange the lights as planned. You'll see that the French windows leading to this terrace are bowed, and have a small balcony over them. After I've gone in, I'll come out to the balcony and you can hand me up the projector and The Brute, which I shall install on the balustrade. At the same time, I'll lower you a lead from the room inside—it's a guest room, fortunately!—so that you can hitch up the junction box and activate the whole works.

"Reeves—you'll find an outhouse across the lawn. Mrs Peel will have left it unlocked. Bring up all the wrought iron garden furniture you can find stacked in there and arrange it here on the terrace, right?

"I shall erect the cyclorama screen and then go in to make certain arrangements and leave these spools of tape in place of those already there. Then I'm going to fix the things on the balcony. And finally—thank God!—Reeves and I will get out of these wet things and we'll all get into drag for the party!... Any questions?"

"Yes." It was Bella speaking. "What about Mrs Peel?"

"I've arranged that with Mr Lurchman. As soon as he possibly can, he's going to try and find out if she's a prisoner here. If he can, and she is—and she's still alive—he's going to give a signal from the study window, which your father will be watching for. And as soon as I get that signal the operation proceeds as arranged. If anything has happened to her, or if she's in immediate danger, he'll give a different signal, and I shall take off on my own. But the rest of you carry on as planned in either case. Any more?"

"Any chance of testing our lights, Mr Steed, before we're *on*, as it were?" Benson asked.

"Absolutely not. *Nothing* must be tried—nothing at all—until we get the word from Lurchman that they've gone under. Then we'll have ten minutes at the most to get the set-up perfect."

"How long do we continue working it? How do we know when to stop?"

"We'll have to play that by ear, Benson. Just carry on. I'll contrive to get any messages necessary to you."

The group broke up and went about its various duties. In a short time the wintry-looking terrace was transformed—insofar as anything could be seen at all before the moon was up. White-painted garden chairs and tables were dotted about in front of the balustrade; exotic plants bloomed by the French windows, down the steps and in a semicircle across the lawn; a length of red-and-white striped blind material with scalloped edges hung down from the balcony—and above it were the arc light and the projector, aimed at the big curve of screen which Steed had erected behind the flowers and shrubs on the lawn. Between this and the balustrade—and indeed on the terrace itself—sub-tropical birds were visible in arrested motion.

Steed, who seemed to have had no difficulty in forcing the lock of the French windows, handed down a length of flex from the balcony, and Benson set about hitching up the light standards to a square, wooden junction box he had stowed at one side of the terrace. The little chauffeur then went through the French windows to where Bella and Reeves were busied about the two suitcases Steed had brought with him in the dinghy. They seemed to be full of clothes.

In a moment, Steed was with them again. Silently, he led Benson from the room, through the hallway of Turret House and up the stairs to the guest bedroom leading on to the balcony. "Since you're the only one not changing," he whispered, "you might as well get settled in now. See you later—I hope!" He left the little man loading film into the projector and stole back downstairs. There was a rumble of voices from behind the closed door to the study, and a crack of light showed below the old-fashioned curtain that hung across it. But neither Charnley nor Warbeck-Simner showed any sign of having heard the trespassers who were violating their privacy.

Of Emma Peel there was no trace at all. Steed searched as far as he dared in the minimal time at his disposal, but the timing of his plan was so critical that it was impossible to pursue the quest. He must simply hope...

Back in the room leading out to the terrace—it was in fact the house's drawing room—he stripped the damp frogman's suit from his body and dropped it on top of the quivering heap that had been Reeves's. From the suitcase, he took a collection of heavy, cream-coloured robes and put them on, adding an arab headpiece which almost completely covered his face when he bent forward. Reeves—now staked out on the far side of the house awaiting Lurchman's signal—should be similarly dressed. Bella had retired to the kitchens to await her cue.

Steed scooped up the rubber suits and the empty valises and stowed them out of sight beyond the terrace. He rolled up the carpet from the drawing room floor and exposed the narrow boards. Then, after removing certain bibelots and rearranging some of the furniture, he went out on to the terrace to wait.

Across the marsh floating on the still air, faintly he heard the clock on Little Hornham church tower striking the quarters, and then the nine solemn strokes of the hour.

As though in answer, there was a burst of sound from the twin exhausts of Mark Lurchman's Jaguar as it drew up by the gates at the far end of the drive. A door opened in the interior and voices called. Footsteps strode through to the front door. Then, probing into the dark sky like fingers, Steed saw through the trees the lights of the E-type moving slowly up the causeway towards the house.

16

A TOUCH OF THE SUN

STEED's plan was bold, simple—and as lunatic as the men it was designed to catch. It consisted of nothing less than tricking them into believing that they were already in North Africa. After which, Steed hoped, they could be persuaded to insert the poison pellets and thus identify the birds they were about to release as messengers of death on their "migration" to Britain!

Lurchman, ostensibly having heard that two old clients were about to go abroad, had telephoned and begged them to accept a case of Champagne as a *bon voyage* gift. He would bring it across himself that evening and crack a bottle with them.

Since they rarely drank, it was reasonable to assume that Mark could fairly easily persuade them to have a little too much —and while they were in that position, he was to introduce into their drinks two small capsules provided by Steed. "Nothing harmful, old boy," the undercover man had assured him. "Just a temporary knock-out drop allied with a mild hallucinogen. The former will give us the required break in time—we could never put it across just taking them as it were from a room in England to a room in Africa, however sloshed they were. But if they *wake up* and find themselves 'in Africa'—well, that's a different thing, isn't it? The memory's never as reliable as a continuous experience. And the hallucinogen?—That's to help them believe what they see, or think they see, when they do wake up."

"How on earth does that work, then?" Mark had asked.

"It's a derivative of *Cannabis Hallucinatrix*—a relative of *Cannabis Indicus* or Marijuana. In this form it doesn't of itself induce specific hallucinations, but it does have the property of making the person under its influence believe—or be more likely to believe—what is *suggested* to him. And I'm hoping that this suggestibility, plus the fact that they'll be a tiny little bit plastered, plus the *trompe l'oeuil* we're going to put on for them, will do the trick . . ."

The optical illusion of course was in reality crude, and wouldn't for a moment have deceived a sane or a sober man.

What Steed was doing, in effect, was to create a film set outside the drawing room windows of Turret House and bring the owners into it. A blaze of arc lamps was to create "sunshine" on the terrace, while carefully deployed props and a projector casting a colour film on to the cyclorama were to sustain the deception. Four factors could upset the illusion: if the "sun blind" hung outside the French windows did not mask the top of the cyclorama screen from the view of those inside the drawing room; if the semi-circle of plants and shrubs did not conceal the junction of the foot of the screen and the lawn; if the two old men at any time realised that the room from which they saw these things was their own drawing room; and if they were unable to get the thing finished before the moon rose. Completely dark surroundings would not obtrude—but moonlight on the marshes would hardly fit in with hot North African sunshine, and middle-distance features in the landscape certainly would show once the moon was up! Similarly, if the striped awning did not hide the top of the screen, whatever scene was shown on it, would apparently be "cut off" half way up the sky . . .

Thinking of all these preparations frantically going on unseen within a few yards of him, Lurchman smiled inwardly as he went through the formalities with his hosts and prepared to open a bottle of Champagne for them. ("Pile it on," Steed had said. "There is no flattery too blatant, no sycophancy too obvious to swell the ego and feed the gullibility of monomaniacs like these!")

"We are distressed indeed, gentlemen," the hotelier said as he poured the frothing liquid into their glasses, "that two such eminent—I was going to say great—men are leaving us, even if only temporarily. I am sure I speak for the rest of my fellow townsfolk when I say: please come back soon—we cannot afford to lose our two most eminent citizens . . . the world's foremost ornithologist and—er—the world's most—er—distinguished scientist!" Feeling slightly ridiculous, he raised his glass to each of the old men in turn. But the exaggerated phraseology and the absurd praise obviously raised no doubts in the minds of his hearers.

"Very civil of you, Lurchman. Very civil," Warbeck-Simner said. "I speak both for my colleague and myself in accepting your good wishes. Your loyalty and that of the townsfolk will be —er—remembered."

Now came the difficult part, Lurchman thought. He tried to

remember the exact words in which Steed had coached him. "It is always a pleasure to associate oneself—however humbly— with men of vision," he said carefully. "And we are only too glad to lend our support—our *unqualified* support—where others have been perhaps ... ungenerous."

"Disloyal," Charnley snapped. "One might almost say treasonable."

"*Treasonable!*" Lurchman gasped in spite of himself.

"Certainly. By rights Sir Albert is the *seigneur* of this district. Failure to show the proper respect can fairly be described as treasonable, I fancy. Especially since Sir Albert's authority will so shortly be so very much—"

"That's enough, Professor, I think," Warbeck-Simner said. "Let me simply say, Lurchman, that those less wise than yourself may soon have cause to regret it."

"A very good thing too," Mark said emphatically. "We have had enough trouble with people not prepared to recognise your —er—greatness. Why only this week—"

"Yes, yes—what were you going to say?"

"Well, there was a busibody—some fellow from London who claimed to be a journalist—who was shooting off his mouth in the local inns in a most disrespectful manner. The villagers soon shut him up and packed him off home with a flea in his ear!"

"Was his name Steed?"

"I believe it was, now that you mention it."

"Ah. I had arranged a lesson, a most salutary lesson, for that impertinent young man—but unfortunately he was blessed with the luck that sometimes attends that kind of beastly insolence, and he ran off."

"Well," Lurchman said, "he's run off altogether now ... And then there was that young woman ..."

"Young woman?" Charnley queried sharply.

"Yes—she was a cousin to Bella Reeves, the poacher's girl, you know. And again—not by any means as respectful as one would wish. Still—I haven't seen her for a day or so. Perhaps she's gone, too."

"Oh, no," Charnley burst out. "*She* hasn't gone—at least not yet, you know—"

"*Charnley!* ... No, the young woman you mention was—is —indeed a cousin of Miss Reeves. She came to work for me for a short while. But, as you rightly say, she was disrespectful as well as being a busibody. I was forced to discipline her. As a matter of fact she's outside now—er—waiting until I decide what to do with her."

"I'm certain that whatever you decide will be just," Mark said, advancing with the Champagne bottle. He prepared to pour.

"No, no, thank you," Warbeck-Simner protested, raising his hand. "We rarely take alcohol, you know—and we have a long journey before us tomorrow."

"At least allow me to toast the confusion of your enemies!"

"Ah, well—if you put it like that. Just a little—no, really. It really is most agreeable of you to bring us this—this libation to attend our wanderings, Lurchman. We shall be grateful to you when we're out there, you know . . . Your good health!"

"And yours, sir," Mark said, raising his glass and wandering over to the windows. Expertly he opened another bottle of Champagne. "Allow me to add a refreshening draught . . ."

"No, no, no, no, no. My dear fellow. Really, we're really not drinkers, you know. Really. No, I insist . . ."

"It's not much use drinking to the downfall of those who would thwart you, if we don't also toast the success of those ventures which should follow their defeat," Lurchman said sententiously.

"A point. That's indeed a point," Charnley said a little thickly. "Don't you feel, my dear Sir Albert—the fellow's right: no earthly use . . . no use at all getting rid of *them* if we don't *succeed!*"

"Perhaps you're right. Well, perhaps just a *little* . . ."

Lurchman poured again, raised his own glass, drank, and placed a cigarette in his mouth. "I hope the weather will keep fine for your flight," he said conversationally. "I think the clouds were finally passing over, as I drove across the marsh. And the wind has definitely dropped . . ." Casually, he raised the curtain and looked out and up at the sky. He produced a lighter from his pocket and lit the cigarette.

"Yes, gentlemen: I think you're all set for a fine day tomorrow," he said, dropping the curtain and moving back into the centre of the room with Steed's four capsules concealed in his hand. "Now—one final sip for the road, as we say: it would be a pity to leave any in the bottle, would it not . . . ?"

Out in the garden, Reeves hurtled round the corner of the terrace and caught hold of Steed's arm. "It's all right," he panted. "Mr Lurchman gave the signal. He lit the cigarette—and he was looking up at the sky. They've swallowed the bait ... and Mrs Peel's still there unharmed ... !"

Steed sighed with relief. "Thank God for that," he said fervently. "Can you hear me, Benson?"

"Loud and clear, Mr Steed," a voice drifted down from somewhere above the striped awning.

"All right, then," Steed called. "I'm nipping upstairs to look out some tropical clothing from our pigeons' luggage while they sleep off their ten-minute Mickey Finns. In the meantime—*Lights! Action! Camera! ...*"

* * *

Raymond Charnley struggled awake. His mouth was dry and there was a slight ache behind his eyes. Really, he felt almost as though he had a hangover! But that was absurd ...

Was it absurd, though? He sat up in the easy chair in which he had been slumped. There was a half full Champagne bottle in a silver bucket just beside him—and on an occasional table by his knee an empty glass. Most puzzling. He looked around him. Warbeck-Simner lay back in a similar chair across the room, his mouth open, snoring. There was a bottle and a glass by him, too. Beyond, double doors opened on to the terrace. The terrace? ... Well, *a* terrace ... On the far side of the shadow cast by the striped sun blind, the warm stones were drenched in heat and light ... Light, light, light shimmered and danced from the blooms of Fuchsia, Bougainvillea, Geranium and Salvia which cascaded over the balustrade and down the steps to the lawn; it gilded the leaves of the tubbed Jasmine whose insidious perfume drifted into the room on the warm breeze; and it scintillated among the jagged spikes of Agave, Yucca and Cactus which fringed the cliff-top at the far end of the hotel garden.

The hotel ...? Charnley rubbed his eyes. *What* hotel, to be sure? He simply could not recall the rest of the place; nor what he had done last night, for that matter. It was all most odd ... He looked out of the window again. Beyond the garden, apparently far below, he saw the sea, blue and intense, stretching sun-dappled to the horizon. Beyond parallel lines of white rollers advancing on the invisible shore, a speedboat towed a water-skier in a vee of foam—and surely that was a felucca sailing slowly towards the ... the what? ... the East? Or the West? ... Charnley shook his head. He was consumed by a great thirst. Reaching for the champagne bottle almost automatically, he poured himself a glassful. To his astonishment, the amber liquid was not the flat and stale souvenir of an evening gone by that he expected: it was ice-cold and sparkling.

"The wine, she is not to your liking, sir?"

A waiter in a white jacket—a squat, wide fellow with bright blue eyes behind a blade of a nose, and a huge black moustache —came into the room from the terrace. He dusted off the white wrought-iron table and chairs set just inside the French windows and looked enquiringly across at the scientist.

"Oh—I—I—why, yes, thank you. Very nice. Very good indeed," Charnley stammered, draining the glass and pouring himself some more. "It's—how long has it been here, d'you know?"

The waiter raised his eyebrows. "Why ten minutes, sir," he said. "Since you ordered it."

"I—er—ordered this Champagne ten minutes ago?"

"But yes—you say she is the only wine to drink before the *petit déjeuner*, so I delay your breakfas' while you drink. The girl bring your coffee and *croissants* in a minute."

Charnley put his hand up to his forehead. Of *course* he had ordered the wine a few minutes ago. He must have done ... yet he couldn't recall actually saying the words. Nevertheless, the waiter was familiar enough. Definitely, he *had* been talking to him a few minutes before. And yet ... and yet ...

Was this the Hotel Armorica in Rabat, where they had booked? Certainly that looked like Mazagan Bay out there— and there was some Arab fellow pottering about among the birds in the garden—There was an Ibis! ... Really his head felt most curious ... Still, it was strange that he couldn't remember the journey at all ... Sir Albert was sitting up and pouring himself a drink.

"Morning, Charnley," he said breezily. "Gorgeous day, isn't it. I must say, I could do with a spot of the jolly old coffee, though. Got a thirst on me like a dredger—this is first-class bubbly, though. Clever of you to think of it."

The ornithologist's hand was unsteady. He spilled a quantity of Champagne down the front of his honey-coloured alpaca jacket. Charnley looked suddenly down at his own clothes. White duck trousers and jacket. Rather creased. They *must* be in Morocco!

There was the tapping of high heels on the terrace. A girl in a black dress with a frilled apron and cap walked up to their table with a tray and begun unloading cups, saucers, cutlery and coffee. "Good morning, gentlemen," she smiled. "I hope you enjoy your little trip last night."

"Little trip?" Warbeck-Simner asked uncertainly. "Last night?"

"But yes. You go to a nightclub in Casbah, no?"

Again, Charnley shook his head. He supposed they must have done. Good God, yes! He could actually hear—beyond the sound of the distant breakers, which he had not noticed until now—the gargling noises of Arab voices raised in argument. There must be a native market place just around the corner. And from the other side of the terrace, carrying clearly on the warm air, the voice of a priest calling the *muzzein* floated. "Most enjoyable," he said, looking at Sir Albert.

The girl poured out coffee. Her hair was looped up in a big chignon and her eyes were heavily made up. From her face—it was quite exceptionally dark—white teeth flashed in a blinding smile. There was something about her that was disturbingly familiar, Charnley felt, eyeing the ripe figure bulging in the tight little dress. Never mind—he would have just one more drink before he tackled the coffee. My word! This Champagne *was* nice... Over the rim of his glass, he watched the girl primp away down the terrace.

Bella had really achieved a remarkable transformation. Now, out of sight around the corner, she stripped off the maid's uniform and revealed herself in a brief two-piece swimsuit of citron yellow satin—an ensemble particularly suited to contrast the rotundities of breast and hip with the concave depths of darkened skin at her waist. Steed approached as she picked up a striped beach towel and slid her feet into sandals. "You're doing splendidly, my dear," he whispered. "Just walk across the garden as though you were expecting to be discovered by a film producer... Yes, Reeves, what is it?"

The poacher was tugging at his sleeve on the other side. "Mr Benson's worried about the time element, sir," he said. "Unless you can create some diversion, the reel will run out in a few minutes and there'll be no more sea and sky until another is loaded."

"I'll do what I can," the undercover man said. "If nothing has happened, tell him to reverse it and run back—I suppose their imagination can stand waves rolling slowly *out* to sea and speedboats towed by water-skiers going backwards! How's the sobriety stakes?"

"The little one's practically on his ear. I'm not sure about the other—he's a funny customer, that one. But they're both digging into the fizz."

Just inside the French windows, Warbeck-Simner and Charnley sat at their table, toying with Champagne, *croissants* and coffee. "I say, there's a dashed attractive gel on her way down to bathe," Sir Albert observed, catching sight of Bella—whose hair now streamed in a dark wave down her back—sauntering across the lawn.

"Yes, yes—most curvac ... curvace ... most agreeable," the Professor giggled. "But look here, don't you think—I mean isn't she—don't you think she's rather like Reeves?"

"Certainly not. She's much taller for one thing."

"Oh, I don't know ... Perhaps one ought to—bit of a closer look, you know. Feel like a bit of a constitu'n'l, don't you? Why'n't we just amble down to the ..." He got up from the table, swaying slightly.

"No, no, Charnley, old boy. You go by all means if you want to. To tell the truth I feel dashed odd this morning ... can't seem to rem'mber anything before—why, I can't even rem'mber getting *up*! ..." He began to laugh: a deep chuckle interspersed with an occasional hiccough. But Charnley was up and away. With an excited cry of "*Look*! Flamingos! In the garden!" he had bounded down the steps and was on the lawn before anyone could move to stop him. As he approached a group of three Flamingos posed before the line of cacti, the Arab gardener who had crossed the lawn earlier moved quickly in his direction. He appeared to be carrying a small billhook. Just before he reached the birds, the scientist appeared to stumble—and an instant later he gave a sharp cry and began to flap one of his hands up and down in the air. "Blasted bird pecked me," he complained, running back up the steps to Warbeck-Simner. "I was only going to have a look ... Blast it!" The back of his hand was bleeding.

"Treacherous birds," the ornithologist said. "Yes, my good fellow? What do you want now?" The waiter was by his side again.

"Excuse me, sir," he said, bowing and turning to the wall. "You do not have your calendar improved for today." He removed the top sheet of a United Arab Airlines daily tear-away calendar.

Warbeck-Simner sat up at the table. He rubbed his eyes. "Good gracious me, Charnley," he exclaimed. "Look! No—

leave your wretched hand alone, man. You're not dying! Look! Look at the *date* . . ."

"I—well, really, I . . . Oh! My goodness! The *birds* . . ."

"Certainly the birds. It's *today*. They must be released!"

"Then let us . . . But just a minute, Sir Albert. Where *are* the birds?"

"Where are they? Why, don't be ridiculous, they're in the . . . in the . . . yes, by gad: where *are* they, indeed?"

"In the la-borrrr-atorr-y, *effendi*: let me show you the way," a tall Arab in burnouse, djellabi and Jermyn Street socks called from the French windows. This was the crucial moment. If either of the two drunken old men thought to query the familiar laboratory in a context of "Moroccan" splendour, the entire exercise was wasted.

But Charnley got up and stood unsteadily by the table without displaying any doubts. "We'd better go, then. Mustn't keep the jolly ol' birds waiting, what!" he cried in slurred tones. "But what about you, my dear S'r Albert? Aren't you coming—or would you like me to—would you like me to cope?"

"No, no, Charnley," Warbeck-Simner waved the scientist away. "I really feel most—*would* you mind? . . . Just to prepare the pellets and slip them in place and . . . and . . . and I'll come along later and see them fly. The Hodder ducks, you know. Just the Hodders . . ." He sank back into his chair and dropped his head into his hands as Charnley shambled off in the wake of the tall Arab. If only his head would stop spinning; if things could stop swinging away from him for a moment . . . And there was a curious, distant whirring noise all the time, which reminded him strongly of something . . . He lifted his head and stared out across the garden. The girl in the swimsuit was walking back towards the terrace. Apparently she hadn't bathed, for her costume was still dry. He watched approvingly as her shadow undulated over the grass, across the spiky leaves of Agave, out over the rollers towards the horizon and then up into the sky . . . *Over the sea and into the sky? A shadow?* Warbeck-Simner leaped to his feet with a shout of fury. "Charnley! Charnley! Stop! Come back!" he screamed. "We've been tricked. There's something wrong . . ."

And at that moment there was a loud snap followed by a hectic slithering, flapping noise, as the entire panorama—waves, sea, sky and shipping—vanished into total darkness.

The film in the projector had broken . . .

17

MRS PEEL PASSES OUT

OF ALL the events in the macabre charade which took place that evening at Turret House, Lurchman was to remember best the moment when Steed made his reappearance on the scene: with his Arab robes held up around his waist like the skirts of a fastidious woman crossing a stream, and his elegantly trousered legs pumping up and down like pistons, the undercover man whistled round the corner of the terrace and sprinted across the lawn in pursuit of Charnley—who had himself clattered into view an instant before in the middle of a flurry of squawking birds. Brightly coloured ducks and drakes were still flapping agitatedly across the flagstones as Steed pelted through the display of stuffed birds and sent them spinning right and left in his wake.

"Stop him!" he called urgently as the scientist streaked across the open space and vanished among the trees on the far side. "He's still got the pellets on him!"

Lurchman and Reeves both moved into action to cut Charnley off, but the little man commanded a fair turn of speed and he was out of sight before they had crossed the area behind the cyclorama screen. Steed waved them down as they reached the edge of the wood between the driveway and the marsh. A false moustache hung drunkenly from one side of his upper lip.

"Leave it," he panted. "We'll have to take it slowly now he's out of sight. Reeves—you're the one with the woodcraft, after all; you follow on after him. If he lies low, wait until he makes a move and then nab him. If he makes a break and goes for the gates—head him off. But keep your mouth shut. Literally. Those pellets are lethal..."

As the poacher melted into the shadows beneath the trees, Steed and the hotelier turned back towards the terrace and the house. "We've got to get to Mrs Peel," Steed said roughly. "From what you tell me, she's probably alright. Probably. But I shan't be satisfied until I'm sure—and until we've got her out of wherever she is ... What we have to do now is to—er—persuade that insane villain to tell us *where*. Either that or—" He broke off suddenly.

The inner door to the drawing room—that stage so carefully set as part of a Moroccan hotel—was swinging open. And through it they saw the mundane hallway of Turret House, with the stairway rising to the upper floors.

But of Sir Albert Warbeck-Simner there was no sign.

"We'd better separate and search the place floor by floor," Lurchman began. He stopped and looked round him. "Where's Bella?" he cried wildly. "Where's Bella gone? My God, if that lunatic has harmed her ..." He dashed from the room and made for the stairs. For the girl, too, appeared to have vanished.

In three strides, Steed was beside him, laying a restraining hand on his arm. "Hold it, Mark," he said quietly. "Nothing to be gained by rushing off without thinking. Let's just recap, shall we? Tell me exactly what happened while I was away?"

"Well, I—I—let's see ... You went off with Charnley to—to get the birds, right?"

"Yes?"

"And then—well, the film broke. At least, I think that's what happened. And the next moment, the madman was on his feet shouting after you and the Professor ... shouting that they'd been tricked, and that he must come back."

"In fact he had tumbled?"

"Yes—but it's odd. For I'm pretty certain that he was on his feet screaming blue murder just *before* the film broke. Bella was walking back across the lawn at the time, I remember."

"He probably saw something that tipped him off. Perhaps he recognised her."

"I don't think so, Mr Steed. But I don't suppose it matters now. Anyway, Charnley came roaring around the corner with you close behind a moment later, so I guess I forgot all about the boss. Until you called me over, that is, and we began to think about it ... What happened over there in the stables, by the way?"

"Well, it was all going to plan, very nicely, as a matter of fact. Pity he had to cotton on just that little bit too soon. We so nearly managed it. Still—I'd done what I meant to. Charnley led me straight to the birds he'd decided to use as his beastly messengers of death: the Hodder ducks ... all crated up ready to go. He went across to the lab to get his poison—one small jar full of the stuff, all ready rolled into pellets."

"Did you find out if that was all there was?"

"Oh, yes—that was more than half the aim of the operation. Otherwise we could just have taken them quietly in yesterday. But we had to get them, not knowing who we were, to show us the extent of the stocks."

"And one jar was all?"

"Yes. Apparently it's very difficult to synthesise—Curare itself is—and he hadn't had so much time since he'd first succeeded in isolating it. This was all he'd had time to make."

"What happened then?"

"Well, apparently it hadn't struck him as odd that, although he was in a hotel in Morocco, he went to the old stables at Bratby to get the ducks—and he was quite happy to accept me as an Arab layabout! Part of the hired help laid on to assist. So he asked me to help him get the ducks out while he put the stuff in place."

"He must have been pretty far gone!"

"On his ear . . . Then I heard Warbeck-Simner yelling his head off—and unfortunately so did the professor. I'd no idea if the—er—facts would percolate through the haze of drink and hallucinogen, so I acted just in case."

"You let the birds loose?"

"Well, shall we say that the crates kind of—er—capsized as I was helping to reach in for the birds? I knew it might tip him off, but I had to get them out of the way: they were the only ones fitted with anklets of the right type, you see. Once they were gone, neither Charnley nor Simner could use any—" He broke off.

A woman's scream had shivered the silence of the huge house. It rose sobbingly into the night air, cracked on a high note and hung eerily in the echoing stairwell.

"Bella!" Lurchman was half way up the stairs before Steed moved.

The girl was standing on the first floor landing, knuckles showing white through the trembling hands bunched under her chin. 'I—I'm sorry," she said weakly. "S-silly of me, I know. B-b-but it was so—so unexpected, you see. And it's . . . oh, so *beastly* in this house!" The hotelier had his arms around her. He caught Steed's glance over Bella's bowed head and flicked his eyes towards a door on the left.

Benson was hidden behind the bed. He was lying on his face with his arms outflung. Blood oozed from a swelling below the grizzled hairs at the back of his head. Steed's probing fingers were gentle. "He'll be all right," he called. "It's a nasty crack but it looks worse than it is. He'll be walking about with a headache and a foul temper in half an hour..."

"But what can we do?" Bella asked.

"We haven't time to do anything. I've laid him on the bed. What happened?"

"Well, when Sir Albert started to shout, naturally I looked up, and I saw him turn round and rush indoors. So, as there wasn't anybody else around, I thought I'd better follow him... but by the time I got upstairs, he'd disappeared."

"That was very courageous of you."

"It wasn't, really. I didn't stop to think. I tiptoed about, and then I heard Sir Albert stamping down the back stairs. I was coming to the window to call you when I tripped over... when I saw..." She gestured to the room where Benson lay.

"I understand. Was Sir Albert carrying anything?—Did you *see* him going down the back stairs?—Did he see you? Did he say anything? Think, Bella."

"He was carrying on like anything, muttering to himself all the time: that's how I finally knew where he was. I saw him rush out of that small store-room near his bedroom with a little bottle in his hand—"

"A bottle?"

"Yes—one of those medicine bottles with grooves down the sides. I don't think he saw me."

"What colour was the bottle?"

"It was dark green. And he was mumbling something about that was that; now he knew what to do. He'd get a syringe and the busibodies—"

"A syringe!" Steed interrupted brusquely. He looked at Lurchman. *"The lab!"* he cried suddenly. *"There's a vivisection theatre at the far end. Come on!"*

Seizing Bella by the arm, he took the stairs two at a time and ran through the kitchens to the back entrance with the hotelier close behind.

They raced across the yard and burst into the long, low building opposite the museum. At the far end was the room which Bella had always thought looked like a small operating theatre. The door was locked.

Steed and Lurchman exchanged glances, then together they hurled themselves at the flush-fitting wood. The door shivered but held. From within came an inarticulate shout of rage. They shouldered it again. And once more the panels shuddered but refused to give way. Lurchman laid a hand on Steed's arm. "Let me," he said quietly—and he withdrew several paces, ran forward, and launched himself at the door with one foot held before him like a battering ram. His heel slammed into the door just below the handle, with all his weight behind it. There was a splintering crash and the door burst open.

Emma Peel lay bent backwards over the steel vivisection table. Her long, slim legs dangled over the edge nearest the door and her arms were drawn down over the sides at the far end. Her wrists and ankles were strapped to the tubular legs. They could not see her face as her head was dropped back over the edge of the small table—but below the pointed chin a pulse was beating faintly. Behind, Warbeck-Simner crouched by an anaesthetic trolley laden with heavy gas cylinders, his eyes wild and furious. In one hand he held a gleaming hypodermic.

"Get away," he snarled. "Keep out of this or it will be the worse for you—and for her." He swung the operating table around on its castored wheels and drew it towards him, thrusting the trolley down towards the door with a push from his foot at the same time. Now that she was broadside on, they could see that Emma appeared to be unconscious.

"By God, Simner," Steed said thickly, "if anything's happened to her..."

He moved forward purposefully into the small room. Mark and Bella stayed one at each side of the door.

"*Stop!*" The ornithologist was behind the vivisection table with its inert human cargo, his syringe held menacingly above her vulnerable neck. "Nothing has happened to her. She's under sedation while I decide how to punish her impertinence." He stared at them balefully, his crazed eyes glittering. "But if you come a step nearer, the needle goes into her throat—and I need hardly specify, Mr Clever Steed, with what the syringe is filled..."

"You dangerous imbecile, *drop that syringe.*" Steed's voice was like a whiplash.

Warbeck-Simner's face crumpled. "You mustn't talk to me like that," he said. "You're supposed to respect me. *I* am the important one here; *I* give the orders. How dare you flout my authority!"

"*Your* authority!" Steed was still advancing slowly, his features a mask of contempt. "The authority of a madman, an outrageous lunatic who has already killed at least sixteen innocent people—for no reason other than the feeding of his own monstrous ego."

"If you mean the fools who died because they ate ducks which had been poisoned by Helimanthine, don't waste your sympathy. They were dispensable. If they were idiot enough to buy illegally poached game, they deserved all they got. It's not my fault if people get hurt poking their noses in—besides, we had to have practical experiments; we couldn't do it *all* on paper: it's not reasonable to expect us to. We had to have a few trial runs before we could justify the expense of taking the birds all the way . . ." He stopped speaking suddenly, his gaze fixed on Steed, who was still wearing the remains of his Arab costume. "Yes," he said softly. "All the way to Morocco. Only we didn't go, did we? Mr Clever Steed was too bright by half: he brought Morocco to us by an underhand, sneaking, despicable, cowardly trick that would have disgraced the lowest guttersnipe in the Civil Service. Well, Mr Brilliant Steed"—his voice, which had been steadily rising as he spoke, now cracked on a note of hysteria and fury— "Well, Mr Brilliant Steed, you're so good at fixing things, see how you can fix *this*!"

With a lightning-like movement, he twitched up the hem of Emma's black skirt to reveal her thighs and plunged the hypodermic needle deep into the soft white flesh which showed above the tops of her stockings.

Before Steed could hurl himself across the room or Mark Lurchman reach the table, he had thumbed home the plunger to inject the contents of the syringe into Emma's veins and swung the wheeled table round to keep it between himself and the two men. Then, with a brusque movement of his arms he shoved it towards them and dodged towards the door. He plucked Bella Reeves away from the doorpost and spun her into the path of Lurchman to confuse the pursuit, and was through the door and away down the long aisles between the laboratory benches before they had realised what he was doing.

Once more Steed took command. "After him, Mark," he cried tightly. "Bring him back alive if you can. But kill him if necessary—like a mad dog, he'll have to be destroyed if he can't be contained." Before Lurchman had wheeled to set off after the madman, he was beside the table, thumbing back Emma's eyelid. His face was very grave.

"All right, Bella," he rapped. "This is up to us. You used to be a nurse. Concentrate—and *remember*. Forget all about the lunatics, forget about what we've been doing, forget about the birds and the marsh. The only thing you must think about is saving Mrs Peel's life. If it's possible, we'll do it."

"What did he inject?" Bella asked.

"Helimanthine, I think. I'm not sure, but we'll have to take a chance—thank God I foresaw something of this kind might happen."

"What can we do?"

"Find me a clean syringe on that rack—No, no. Don't bother to sterilise it. We haven't time." He reached into his pocket as the girl ranged along the wooden fixture, seeking a hypodermic of suitable size, and took out a small phial.

"That'll do," he called. "Hand it over. Quick. Right."

He snatched the gleaming instrument from her hand and jabbed the needle upwards into the rubber bung of the inverted phial.

"What is it, Mr Steed?" Bella asked as he withdrew the plunger to fill the syringe.

The undercover man was pinching up a fold of flesh in the bend of Emma's elbow. "Prostigmine," he replied without looking up. "It's the antidote to Curare—and Helimanthine's a more powerful derivative of Curare—so I'm hoping that it may work."

"Suppose it wasn't Curare that he gave her? What effect will the antidote have?"

Steed plunged home the piston and held the hypodermic in place. "I don't know," he said soberly. "I just don't know."

He straightened up, handing the syringe back to Bella. "Now we have to work," he said. "Do you know the effect of Curare?"

"Only that it relaxes you. They use it in surgery sometimes."

"It relaxes by completely paralysing the muscles, so that you've no control over them whatever, conscious *or unconscious*. In minute doses this helps surgeons: it stops patients under anaesthetic from involuntarily contracting their muscles while incisions are made. But in large doses it's fatal because it stops the muscles of the heart and lungs working and the victim suffocates."

"What does the antidote do?"

"I don't know," Steed said frankly. "All I know is that it acts fairly quickly, but that you've got to give it time to chase round the circulatory system until it catches up, as it were, the poison. Then it has a chance to do its work." He had been anxiously watching Emma's face as he spoke, and now he leaned down and scrutinised her features. "Bella," he said sharply. "One of those trolleys must carry oxygen cylinders. Please locate it and bring it over."

The girl darted over to the opposite wall, spinning the rejected trolleys out of the way as she sought the one Steed required. "Nitrous Oxide," she muttered, "Chloral Hydrate, Ether, Chloroform—surely there must be . . . Ah! It's the one he shoved at the door!" She wheeled the heavy carriage with its twin cylinders and corrugated loops of rubber tubing over to Steed.

"We'll have to use this, Bella," he said tensely. "The drug's acting too quickly. Look—the breathing's getting shallower and shallower. The muscles of the lungs are packing up."

"Shall I untie her hands and feet?"

"No. We haven't time. Put the mask over her face. Quick— we'll have to help her breathe until the antidote's had time to work." In the silence of the laboratory, the rubber bag beneath the face mask filled and emptied itself pathetically slowly, the creases in the quartered container inflating and deflating with a desultory pop. Soon, the flow of breath was reduced to a flutter.

"More oxygen," Steed said tightly. "The movement of the lungs has practically stopped . . . Bella—watch the rhythm of her breathing and take over."

"What do you mean?"

"Reverse the tap so that the gas fills the bag, and then force it into the lungs by squeezing the bag with your hands . . . yes, that's it. Slowly. Keep the same rhythm as the breathing . . . Good. Keep her going while I give her another injection of Prostigmine . . ."

Intent about their tasks, the man and the girl busied themselves around the inert figure on the operating table. As Bella palped the breathing bag and kept the mask firmly jammed over Emma's unconscious face, Steed leaned his weight on and off her rib cage, willing the paralysed lungs to work in time with the incoming oxygen. At last there was a tremor, an answering movement beneath his hands. The marbled eyelids shivered; the nostrils dilated. There was a faint rattling at the back of the throat as air began to be drawn back into the mouth.

The antidote was beginning to work.

Several things happened at once then. There was a sudden confused noise of shouting outside the building. Footsteps pounded on the cobbles of the yard. Clearly into the night air the sound of two shots reverberated—the flat, ringing crack of an automatic followed by the deeper boom of a shotgun. Steed sprang for the door. "Look after her, Bella," he called. "She should be all right now—but keep a close watch. I must go out and help . . ."

He sprinted through the laboratory and out into the open air. The moon was up now, etching ebony shadows behind the pale, flat cutouts of turret and wall. On the terrace and across the lawn, the debris of the evening's masquerade was strewn oddly in the silver light. Someone had put out the arc lights and these, like metal birds roosting on their gantries, presided over the tangle of cables on which stuffed Flamingos and live ducks lay scattered and bemused. At one corner of the balustrade, Reeves crouched, the barrel of his duck gun glinting in the moonlight.

He was facing the yard, head cocked forward and eyes strained to pierce the shadows at the foot of the steps. And round the corner of the house behind him—having circled the building undetected—Charnley stole step by step across the flags with a pistol at the ready.

Before Steed could open his mouth to shout a warning, there was a blur of movement from the balcony above the scientist's head, and something dark and amorphous swept down to envelope his head and shoulders in its folds. The poacher swung round and closed with the struggling man, his long arm tweaking the gun from his adversary's grasp before Charnley realised what had happened. There was a brief tussle on the terrace, but by the time Steed had run up the steps to lend a hand, Reeves had the scientist in an arm lock and the battle was over. "Thanks, mate," the poacher called, panting, with a glance upwards at the balcony. And then Steed saw that Benson, recovered from the blow which had knocked him out, was leaning over the edge by the silent projector.

"Have you seen the other one, Benson?" Steed asked.

"Not a sign, Mr S . . . Came to after that crack on me nut and looked out to see Reeves and Dr Who down there doin' a duel in the moon, and that's all. I did hear footsteps—*There he is!*"

The little man was pointing excitedly towards the drive. Reeves swung the captive Charnley, still with the coat Benson had dropped over his head, in that direction and they all stared towards the front of the house. The substitute tape recordings Steed had lodged earlier in the evening were still relaying the sounds of waves breaking and oriental voices bargaining in the market. Against this bizarre background Warbeck-Simner's appearance was lent a grotesque quality which momentarily froze them to the spot.

The master of Turret House was dressed in full peer's regalia, ermine robes and all. A coronet sat rakishly upon his domed head. There was some kind of mayoral chain of office around his neck and in his hand he carried what looked remarkably like a mace. In the bright moonlight he strode towards the house gesturing with his free hand, his eyes glaring and his lips flecked with foam.

"Strewth!" Benson said from above. "He's gone right round the bend now... off his rocker completely!"

"I think we're seeing the first appearance of the new Earl of Bratby—and probably the Gauleiter of all England in his own crazy mind," Steed murmured. "He's going to get a bit of a shock, though, if he comes much further."

"What, them white posts with the magic eyes?"

"Yes—but they won't actuate a tape of dogs barking. I—er—altered the programme for tonight..."

Warbeck-Simner was approaching the double row of posts. Before he reached them, Charnley twisted eel-like from Reeves's grasp, threw off the coat, and dashed towards his chief. "My lord," he was shouting, "your humble subjects prepare to demonstrate their loyalty..."

Warbeck-Simner passed the first pair of white posts.

There was a screech of multiple jets, the roar of a heavy aircraft diving immediately overhead. The noise was appalling.

The ornithologist halted in his tracks, gave one terrified glance upwards—and then broke for the cover of the trees. At the other end of the line of posts Charnley, too, stared at the deafening noise in the sky before running in panic from the road. On converging diagonals, the two madmen rushed towards each other through the bushes.

"*Simner! Stop,*" Steed cried suddenly, starting forward. "*Look out, you fool. Charnley's going to run across—*"

He broke off. The roar of the tape-recorded airplane died away in the distance, and clearly in the ringing silence which replaced it they heard the squeak of the gate as Charnley hurled himself through the wicket. There was a dreadful, vibrant twang and the crash of something heavy among the Rhododendrons. Then the scientist's footsteps receding among the dead leaves under the trees.

Steed and Reeves hurried across the drive as Benson ran down the stairs inside the house to join them. Warbeck-Simner lay on his face. The murderous bolt from the crossbow had caught him between the shoulder blades and now only the tip of the steel shaft gleamed incongruously in the bright moonlight above the crumpled crimson of his robe. Below him, a deeper crimson seeped stealthily among the leaves.

* * *

It was a half hour later. Emma had quite recovered and was sitting in one of the wrought iron chairs by the French windows, with Bella standing protectively behind her. Steed, Benson and the poacher were sampling a bottle of brandy which Reeves had found in the dining room cupboard, and Mark Lurchman was standing guard over a sullen Charnley. The scientist had run full tilt into him while he was still trying to locate Warbeck-Simner and the struggle which followed had been short but decisive. The jar of poison pellets stood isolated in the centre of the table.

The body of the master of Turret House had been decently recovered and now, as they waited for the police to arrive from Bratby, they looked at each other wondering what to say.

The six of them presented an odd sight: Bella with a bath robe flung over the yellow bikini and her darkened flesh; Steed and the poacher still swarthy beneath their Arab robes; Mark wearing a white jacket and a false moustache; Benson in ordinary clothes—and Emma looking prim and proper in the black and white uniform of a housemaid ...

It was Emma who broke the silence first. She burst out laughing. "Well, I don't know about Double-Oh-Seven," she said, "but if this was an espionage operation, at least we could claim to be the Double-Ee-Three!"

"I'm sorry to be slow on the uptake, my dear," Steed said, looking at her dubiously, "but I don't quite..."

"You and Bella and myself," Emma said, laughing weakly again. "Steed, Reeves, Peel—the three names, don't you see? They all have double ee ... Oh, never mind! Perhaps Helimanthine makes you light headed..."

"It's not that, miss." It was Benson speaking. "There's a perfectly good reason here for the whole shoot. Look!"

He was pointing to the calendar which Mark had altered to show the date on which the Hodder ducks were due to leave Morocco. The heavy black lettering spelled out the words *APRIL 1st*.

18

YOU CAN ALWAYS DUCK...

"PRETTY gel. Got a fine pair of legs on her." His Nibs was not noted for the prodigality of his praise when the distaff side was under review. Across the low table General Mackinlay lay back in his armchair and nodded his head several times.

"Aye," he said at last.

"I mean to say, I don't hold with all this modern flummery and women drivin' motors an' all that. But young Steed's at least picked a gel to help him on this do who knows how to hold herself. Bet she's a tolerable seat on a horse, too."

"Aye."

"Mind you, Mackinlay, these things are best left to men. But I'm not saying she wasn't of use. We'd never have known about their batty plans at all if she hadn't been staked out inside the place, would we?"

The general leaned forward and lifted his glass of whisky from the table. He sipped and considered. "No," he said at length. "No, ye would not indeed."

His Nibs reflected a moment longer on their recently departed guests. "All the same," he said, "I shall never really understand these young people. Just look at their behaviour at luncheon." He picked up his own glass and drained it.

"Ye're no suggestin', forbye—"

"I'm suggesting nothing, Mackinlay. But you'd think after all that gadding about in the open air that they'd have worked up something of an appetite, wouldn't you?—Not a bit of it. They left practically all of that duck pâté. Both of them. Extraordinary people! I'm surprised at young Steed..."

He picked up his copy of *The Times* and rattled it disapprovingly.

"It's all finished, then? Ye'll no be needin' the platoon I was offerin' ye?"

"No, no, thank you very much, Mackinlay. MacCorquodale's men have combed the place out and taken away all the interesting stuff from the lab. The poison's accounted for and so are all the birds. Charnley'll get ten years on the conspiracy charge alone. It's all over now, thank God."

"Aye... 'Twas a queer case just the same. A weird one."

"Nonsense, Mackinlay." His Nibs settled down behind his paper once more. "Not half so queer as some of the things these newspaper fellers would have us believe." His voice growled on petulantly. "What do they take us for? A lot of blessed idiots or what?... Just listen to this—here's some feller says an *eagle* has been seen over the beach at Ostend carrying an umbrella ... I mean, I ask you! An eagle. With an *umbrella*!"

"At Ostend?"

"Yes... I daresay you're right there, Mackinlay. They're a pretty odd lot, these continentals. Even so, fancy expecting us to believe a story like that..."